Penny Jordan

THE RELUCTANT SURRENDER

PARENTI
DYNASTY

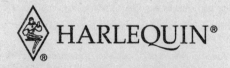

HARLEQUIN®

TORONTO • NEW YORK • LONDON
AMSTERDAM • PARIS • SYDNEY • HAMBURG
STOCKHOLM • ATHENS • TOKYO • MILAN • MADRID
PRAGUE • WARSAW • BUDAPEST • AUCKLAND

Recycling programs
for this product may
not exist in your area.

ISBN-13: 978-0-373-12963-8

THE RELUCTANT SURRENDER

First North American Publication 2011

Printed in U.S.A.

All about the author…
Penny Jordan

PENNY JORDAN has been writing for more than twenty-five years and has an outstanding record: over 165 novels published, including the phenomenally successful *A Perfect Family,* *To Love, Honour and Betray, The Perfect Sinner* and *Power Play,* which hit the *Sunday Times* and *New York Times* bestseller lists. She says she hopes to go on writing until she has passed the 200 mark, and maybe even the 250 mark.

Although Penny was born in Preston, Lancashire, U.K., where she spent her childhood, she moved to Cheshire as a teenager, and has continued to live there. Following the death of her husband, she moved to the small traditional Cheshire market town, on which she based her Crightons books.

She lives with a hairy Birman cat—Posh—who assists her with her writing. Posh sits on the newspapers and magazines that Penny reads to provide her with ideas she can adapt for her fictional books.

Penny is a member and supporter of both the Romantic Novelists' Association and the Romance Writers of America—two organizations dedicated to providing support for both published and yet-to-be-published authors.

CHAPTER ONE

As SHE turned into the underground car park, shared by
the architectural practice she worked for with several
other businesses in the same modern block, Giselle saw
a car reversing from one of the precious spaces. Quickly
she turned the wheel of her small company car against
the arrows, driving up an exit lane, her brain and body
automatically focusing on getting to the empty space
before anyone else spotted it. She only realised as she
swung round the end of the exit lane and up to the space
that an imposing, expensive, polished sports car, with
an equally imposing, expensive and polished, far too
harshly good-looking man at its wheel, was stationary
just down from the space. He had obviously been waiting for the space's occupant to leave.

He looked at her, his expression one of arrogance
mingled with open male disbelief. For a second she
hesitated, her resolve almost failing, but then she saw
how his glance moved deliberately from her face to her
body, as though she was a piece of merchandise he was
looking over and then rejecting, and a spurt of pure
female fury had her turning into the spot for which he
had been waiting.

She could see the cold savagery of the look he was

giving her, and lip-read the words, *What the hell—?* as they were formed by the sensually chiselled hard male mouth as she swept past him, her whole body shaking, her hands damp with perspiration as she clung to the wheel.

It wasn't just because his arrogance had infuriated her that she was doing this. This morning she'd received an unexpected call asking her to get to the office early, to be present after the senior partners' meeting. She could not afford to be late; necessity overruled and squashed the guilt she would normally have felt at her lack of good road manners. Then he had given her that look—that assured, arrogant, hateful glance at her body—that had said so clearly exactly what kind of man he was: predatory, callous, completely fixated on his own desires and needs.

Her need for the parking space was far greater than his, Giselle told herself. She had to be in the office—fifteen minutes ago. He, on the other hand, looked the sort who normally had a driver to attend to such mundane things as parking his car.

Inside the car, she started to change her driving shoes for her office heels. The sound of an engine revving furiously made her exhale in relief. He had obviously driven away—at high speed and in high dudgeon, no doubt.

Having moved his car a few yards, to let another vehicle pass him, Saul Parenti stared with furious disbelief at the thief who had just taken his parking spot. The fact that this deed had been commited by a woman added insult to injury. Saul had the blood of generations of powerful men running through his veins—men in control, in authority, absolute rulers—and right now that blood was running very hot and fast indeed. Saul would never have described himself as a misogynist, far from it—he liked women. He liked them a lot. But generally speaking the place where he liked them most was in his bed—not in a parking spot for which he had been waiting with a patience that went against his nature.

With no other parking space available, he parked swiftly to one side, obstructing two vehicles, and switched off the car engine. He pushed open the door, unfolding his muscular six-foot-four length from the driving seat of his car.

Giselle was unaware that her theft was about to be challenged until she was out of her small car. Making the short walk from the car park to the lift that would take her up to the office was the time she normally used to get her professional mask firmly in place—the one that hid the fact that she disliked the male interest so often directed at her at work. Because of this she was too involved in adopting her cloak of defensive hauteur—straight back, straight-ahead focus, and a lift of her chin that said she was untouchable—to be aware of the danger until it was too late and she was forced to rock back on her heels in mid-stride or risk walking straight into the man standing between her and the exit.

'Not so fast. I want a word with you.'

His English was excellent, and somehow slightly at odds with his darkly male looks.

Well, she certainly did not want to exchange any words with *him*. Giselle stepped past him, and then gasped in outraged shock when he blocked her, stepping closer to her, until she felt as though each breath was filled with the raw masculine smell of him—all dark, erotic mastery spiked with something sharper, like the touch of a velvet glove spiked with hidden danger.

'You're in my way,' she told him as she fought to keep and sound cool—not realising the dangerous opening she had given him.

'And you are in my parking spot,' he retorted.

That might be true, but she wasn't about to give it or anything else up to him.

'Possession is nine-tenths of the law,' she quipped, and then wished that she hadn't when he seemed to move even closer, his presence somehow paralysing and imprisoning her.

'Possession belongs to those who are strong enough to take what they want and hold on to it—whether that applies to a parking space—or a woman.'

And he was a man who *would* possess *his* woman. The knowledge of that had somehow got under her protective armour, and now that it had... She was beginning to feel dizzy, weak, filled with a febrile excitement brought on by the clash of words between them, a dangerous desire to go on pushing him, to test his self-control.

A shudder ripped though her. This was madness. Just because he was a man. And *what* a man, she was forced to acknowledge dizzily. For a start there was his height—easily over six feet, so that even in her heels she had to tilt her head back to look up at him. Somehow, despite the fact that she had worked for years never to allow herself to be physically aware of men, this one had such a powerful aura of raw male sexuality about him that she suspected it would be impossible for *any* woman not to be aware of him. Her own unexpected and unwanted vulnerability set off a chain reaction of panic and anger inside her, and those emotions were intensified by the fact that they could not block out the effect his maleness was having on her.

Unfamiliar and definitely unwanted thoughts were springing up inside her head with such vigour that it was impossible for her to cull them. Dangerous thoughts, all allied to the fact that he was a man. And not *just* a man but the architectural equivalent of instant visual gratification via the perfection of the design of his outer form. In fact looking at him could easily become a female compulsion, Giselle suspected helplessly. That expensive-looking shirt he was wearing must surely have been made to measure for him, to cover those shoulders and that chest. No surplus fat there. His body looked as though it would be all hard muscle over silken flesh. How would it feel to touch such a man? What would it be like to have such a feast of male sensuality spread out for her delight and the enticement of her senses? A quiverful of molten aching darts of longing were piercing her body, lethally infecting it with tiny stings of desire.

Protectively Giselle lifted her hand to her heart in an attempt to steady its increased beat. She must *not* feel like this. Not now and not ever. Not for this man or for any man. She tried to look away from him, to break the spell his sexuality had cast over her, but instead her gaze slid recklessly to his face and became enmeshed there.

His genes were not derived from any Anglo-Saxon ancestor, she was sure. Not with those arrogant, almost

Roman Byzantine features, with that hint of cruelty stamped into them. No. His was an intensely masculine face—intelligent, educated, arrogant and elegant. The Mediterranean olive flesh was drawn smoothly against high cheekbones, a strong jaw, and the Roman strength of his nose. If it hadn't been for his unexpectedly silver eyes she would have said that this was a man whose bloodline came from the darkest mists of time—from a race of men destined by birthright and their own strength to sweep aside all opposition to their will.

One blast from those grey eyes was like having a laser gun applied to her icy shield. This was a man with a capital M—all-male, all-powerful, a man who believed that his will, his needs and desires should be free to rove and take possession of whatever they and he wanted.

The shock of being confronted by him was definitely having a dangerous effect on her. Somehow her senses had managed to break through the mental chastity belt in which she normally locked them to behave like a group of hormone overloaded teenagers, all too ready to feast themselves on the banquet in front of them. Only of course she had no intention of allowing them to do any such thing. And she had years of practice in ensuring that they obeyed her, she reminded herself as she struggled to retain her air of icy uninterest.

She didn't like him, Giselle decided. She didn't like him one little bit. He was far too arrogant. And far too male for her own comfort. Was that why she didn't like him? Because she knew instinctively that his brand of male sexuality was very dangerous to her and that she was not as protected from it as she knew she had to be? Of course not, she assured herself determinedly.

Saul studied the woman standing in front of him with a practised male gaze. Medium height, slim—although the combination of the almost uniform-like dullness of her black skirt suit, worn over a plain white shirt, and the fact that her clothes were cheap and ill-fitting, as though they were a size too big for her, made it impossible to judge accurately how feminine her body shape might be. Her blonde hair was drawn back tightly into a smooth chignon that revealed the delicate bone structure of her face, with its femininely pronounced cheekbones and luminous skin. The gold tips to her eyelashes revealed by the overhead lighting suggested that they were neither dyed nor covered in mascara. Some men might find her cool, touch-me-not Grace Kelly-type looks a sexual challenge, and be curious enough to see just how much applied male interest her ice would take before cracking, but he was not one of them. He liked his women subtly and seductively wanton and willing—not playing at being ice maidens so that they could demand their ice was melted.

However, even if she had been his type, right now his attention was focused on retribution rather than seduction.

'Let me past,' Giselle demanded, asserting herself in an attempt to remind herself of the reality of the situation.

Her sharp demand added to Saul's impatient fury. She had stolen his parking space, and she was argumentative, stubborn, and refusing to admit that she was in the wrong. Her whole attitude made him want to put her in her place.

He wasn't going to move, and she was going to be

late. Determined to make her escape, Giselle stepped quickly to one side of him—but as she did so he reached for her, taking hold of her forearms in a fiercely hostile grip. She could feel their bruising pressure on her flesh, male and alien and burning away the layers of cloth between them, so that it was almost as though he was touching her bare skin. A shocking sensation seized hold of her body as powerfully as he seized hold of her, panicking her into curling her hands into fists that she wanted to beat against his chest.

'Let me go,' she insisted furiously.

Let her go? There was nothing he wanted to do more. She'd already caused him more trouble in five short minutes than he'd ever allowed any woman to cause him. He looked directly at her. Her face was white and set, her eyes burning with temper, her mouth...

Still holding her with one hand, he removed the other from her arm to reach up and very deliberately wipe the lipstick from her mouth with his thumb, as if in preparation to kiss her.

She stood frozen, shocked at the intimate gesture, and the moment stretched as their gazes locked. Unable to move, Giselle was stunned by the leap of sensation his gaze shifting to her mouth conjured within her, and with it the hunger to—to what? To lean in to him?

The sudden blaring of a car horn close to them had Saul releasing his prisoner, thrusting her away from him as he did so. What had possessed him? And what would have happened if they hadn't been disturbed? he asked himself as Giselle took advantage of the interruption to run from him.

To Giselle's relief he didn't follow her to the

lift—which thankfully was empty. In it, on the way up to her office, with her heart thudding and racing and her mind in turmoil, she had to force herself not to think about what had just happened but instead to focus on the reason everyone had been called into the office.

For the past two years—in fact virtually since she had joined the prestigious practice of architects—the firm had been working on a lavish and costly project for a Russian billionaire, which involved turning a small island he had acquired off the coast of Croatia into a luxury holiday resort for the very wealthy. The financial downturn had led to the project being put on hold, much to the dismay of the firm's senior partners, but then late yesterday they had received news that the island had a new owner, in the shape of another billionaire—a very successful entrepreneur, who had seen the plans for the island and now wanted to discuss them.

This news had galvanised the senior partners into swift action. Everyone connected with the plans—no matter in how lowly a capacity—had been instructed to make themselves available after the preliminary early-morning meeting, in case the island's new owner wished to discuss any aspect of the plans with them. The hope was that he would give the green light to the stalled project, but of course there was no guarantee of that. With the threat of potential redundancies looming over them, naturally the more junior architects, like Giselle, were keeping everything crossed that he would look favourably on the plans.

The lift had stopped at her floor. Giselle exited the lift and headed for the office she shared with several other junior architects—all of them male, apart from her, and all of them in their different ways determined to show both her and the senior partners that they were a better financial investment for the firm than she could ever be.

'It's all right,' said Emma Lewis, their shared PA, as Giselle stepped into the office. 'The meeting's been put back an hour. Apparently the new owner has been unavoidably delayed.'

Giselle exhaled with relief and told her, 'I thought I was going to be late. I had to come in my car, because I've got a site meeting this evening, and the traffic was appalling.'

Emma, thirty-four to Giselle's twenty-six, and married to a surveyor who was working on a contract out in the United Arab Emirates, treated her juniors in much the same way as she did her two children—mothering them with fond affection and doing her best to break up any quarrels between them. Giselle liked her, and was very grateful for the support Emma gave her.

'Where's everyone else?' Giselle asked Emma, only to groan and go on, 'No, don't tell me—let me guess. They're all in the gents, trying to work out how to avoid any blame that might be handed out whilst claiming any plaudits that could be going.'

Emma burst out laughing.

'Something like that, I expect. I'll bring you coffee, and then I'll tell you the latest I've heard about our possible new client.'

Giselle nodded her head, and tried not to grimace inwardly. If Emma had one fault it was that she was devoted to gossip magazines charting the lives of the rich and famous, and Giselle suspected that 'the latest' was probably going to be some kind of information she'd gleaned from the pages of one of those dubious sources.

Five minutes later, sipping her coffee whilst she listened to Emma, she knew that she was right.

'I'd never have seen it if I hadn't had to take Timmy to the dentist, because the magazine was months old, and I couldn't believe it when I opened it and right in front of me was an article about Saul Parenti. You'd think he was Italian with that surname, wouldn't you? But he isn't. Apparently his family actually own their own *country,* and his cousin is its Grand Duke. It's somewhere near Croatia, and only small, but apparently he—Saul Parenti, I mean—is fabulously wealthy in his own right, apart from being the cousin of a duke, because his father was involved in loads of business deals with the middle East.'

'Fascinating.' Giselle applauded obligingly.

'I just love knowing all about people's backgrounds and their families, don't you?' Emma enthused. 'His mother was American, and high up in one of the overseas aid agencies. She and his father were killed in South America whilst she was working there, in the aftermath of an earthquake.'

Giselle nodded her head, to show she was following Emma's story, but inwardly the last thing she felt like doing was listening to gossip. Her comment about the death of Saul Parenti's parents had caused an all too familiar panicky swell of nausea and defensive fear to rise insidiously inside her.

The door to the office opened to admit one of the other junior architects, Bill Jeffries. Stockily built and confident, he swaggered into the office looking pleased with himself. Bill considered himself to be something of a ladies' man. He had made advances to her when she had first joined the practice.

Because she had rebuffed him, she was now on the receiving end of increasing animosity and sexual hostility towards her, and Giselle knew perfectly well what he was getting at when he gave a fake shiver and protested, 'Brr…it's cold in here!' before pretending to notice her and then saying, 'Oh, sorry—I hadn't seen you there, Giselle.'

Giselle said nothing. She was well accustomed to Bill's malice and baiting, which she knew sprang from the fact that she had so resolutely refused all the attempts of both him and the other men she worked with to flirt when she had first joined the practice. Bill had chosen to take her chilly manner personally, and she had no intention of telling him that, far from being personal, her icy reserve was a defensive mechanism she used against *every* man who attempted to show any kind of sexual interest in her. If Bill and other men like him chose to be offended because she didn't welcome their attentions, then so be it. The truth was that a long time ago she had sworn that she would never allow herself to date men—because dating could lead to falling in love, falling in love led to making a commitment, and making a commitment led in turn to becoming a pair, and from that pair would come children…

'Bill, I've just been telling Giselle what I've read about Saul Parenti.' Emma broke the hostile silence. 'Giselle, I still haven't told you everything. Apparently he's fabulously wealthy, with a reputation for driving a very hard bargain where his business and his romantic interests are concerned. When it comes to women he likes to play the field—he's supposed to be a wonderful lover—but he's said publicly that he never intends to marry.'

'Hear that, Miss Ice Queen?' Bill mocked Giselle. 'Sounds like our new client is just the man to get you warmed up so that you'll drop your knickers.' He gave an unpleasant snicker. 'Mind you, I don't envy him if he does—all that ice would freeze the balls off any man.'

'Bill!' Emma protested.'

'Well, it's true,' he said, unabashed.

'It's all right, Emma,' Giselle assured the PA. 'My chosen profession is architecture, Bill,' She pointed out calmly. 'Not prostitution.'

'You mean it is if you can keep your job. And, let's face it, you certainly won't win any commissions with your female wiles,' he sneered in response.

'I don't need to use *any* wiles, female or otherwise, to keep my job,' Giselle couldn't resist coming back at him pointedly, causing him to colour up angrily.

Bill was one of those employees who liked to play the good team player in front of those he thought it would impress, whilst being very much a person who put himself first. Bill liked to use their shared gender to get the other men in the office on side with him, and to exclude her, but Giselle had never seen any real evidence that he was the team player he liked to claim he was.

In the senior partners' office the atmosphere was thick with a mixture of tension and determination—the tension coming from Mr Shepherd, one of the senior partners, and the determination from Saul Parenti, the man he needed to satisfy that his firm was up to the challenge being set.

'Yes, of course I accept that you wish to meet and speak with the team who will be working on the changes to the plans you have requested. Perhaps lunch with the other senior partners involved in the plans?'

'I wish to meet *everyone* involved in the project— senior and junior,' Saul stressed briskly.

He did not have time to waste. He was already running late, thanks to the woman who had stolen his parking space and a telephone call from his cousin. Aldo, five years his junior and recently married, might be Grand Duke of Arezzio, thanks to the fact that his father had been their grandfather's eldest son, and his own the younger, but he still turned to him when he needed financial advice. Saul shrugged inwardly. He had done his best to help his young cousin build up some reserves for the royal coffers of Arezzio, the small country on what had once been the border between the old Austrian Empire and Croatia, but Aldo was not a businessman—he was more of an academic. He did not like the harsh cut and thrust of modern business, and preferred to spend his time cataloguing the rare books in the library of his castle in Arezzio.

Saul was grateful for the fact that his father had not been the elder brother, and that he had been spared the onerous duty of becoming Arezzio's Grand Duke, being forced to marry and produce an heir. He might not have approved when Aldo had married Natasha, because he didn't think Natasha loved his cousin, but he would be very pleased when their marriage produced the child that would mean that he would be not just one but two steps removed from the Dukedom. He was, he believed, like his mother. Like her, he loved the excitement and adventure of new challenges and demands on his energy. Her life had been her aid work. She had loved his father, and no doubt she had loved him too, but parenting a child had not been the focus of his mother's life.

His own view now was that it would be wrong for him to bring a child into the world when he knew how little time he would have for it. He was driven in his work, in his need to explore the outer boundaries of creating the most exciting and enticing of luxurious holiday destinations which at the same time supported the environment and the local population. It was a purpose to which his emotional time as well as his physical time was given over wholly. He would not have a child and leave it to be raised by others, and he did not need or want an heir. When the time came for him to hand over the business he would find the right hands to hold it safe.

Given all that, financing his cousin—and thus in part the country itself—was a small price to pay for his personal freedom.

A personal freedom he never intended to relinquish, either via a public commitment or a private one—of any kind.

Saul could see the senior partner of the architectural firm who had been commissioned to design the complex its previous owner had planned to create on the island did not approve of Saul's demand. It always irritated him when people failed to grasp why he made the decisions he did and delayed executing the orders that related to those decisions. Their failure betrayed a lack of vision and foresight, as well as poor financial acumen. Which was no doubt why the firm was on the point of bankruptcy—or would have been if he hadn't just confirmed that he intended to keep them on and go ahead with the redevelopment of the island.

At the back of his mind was the thought that, should he increase his financial interest in such projects, adding an architectural practice to his portfolio of business holdings would be financially beneficial. For now, though, he intended to make it plain that he would *not* be paying them the kind of fees they had previously anticipated, and he would be keeping a far tighter control of both budgets and plans for the venture. Taking and keeping control was why he was a billionaire, with his fortune growing every day, whilst other rich men were losing money.

'I wish to see them all because I want to make it clear to them that from now on it is *my* instructions they will be following and *my* approval they must win,' he informed the senior partner. 'The previous plans were spouting wasted money like a leaking colander.'

'Our original brief was that no expense be spared,' Mr Shepherd protested defensively.

Saul gave him a cool look.

'Which is no doubt why one of your junior staff elected to have the floor of a summerhouse that is open to the weather tiled in handmade tiles that are not frost-proof.'

'An error which of course would have been picked up,' the senior partner assured him.

'Of course. But I prefer those who work for me not to make such errors in the first place.' Saul looked at his watch, and this time the senior partner stood up.

'I believe all our staff are in the building. I will arrange for all those who worked on the plans to be summoned,' he said unwillingly.

'I have a better idea,' Saul told him. 'Why don't you show me round the office instead, and introduce me to them that way?'

It often paid to see what people were working on. Fortunes could be built—and destroyed—by such means.

The whisper had spread through the office. 'The project's going ahead and he's keeping us on.' And naturally everyone's mood was upbeat and buoyant, with all the staff relieved to have the worry of the last couple of months, when they hadn't known whether or not they would end up being made redundant, finally removed.

Giselle was as relieved as everyone else. She'd worked hard to get where she was, to qualify for and get a job that would enable her to support herself all through her adult life—because she *would* have to support herself. She knew that. There would never be a man, a partner, a husband who loved her and whom she loved in turn to share the burden of providing a roof over their head with her. How could there be when—?

The door to their office opened, and everyone fell silent as Mr Shepherd, one of the senior partners, came in—an unheard-of event. But it wasn't the sight of him that had driven the colour from Giselle's face, leaving it bleached of colour as she stared into the face of the man accompanying him.

It was the man from the car park. The man whose space she had stolen—the man who was now their most important client, Giselle recognised as she heard the senior partner introduce him.

'Mr Parenti wishes to meet all those who have worked or will be working on the plans for the island project,' the senior partner announced.

'Saul,' their new client corrected the older man. 'Not Mr Parenti.' Respect, as far as he was concerned, was something that was earned, not bestowed, and he had no doubt at all about his ability to earn the respect of others.

Whilst he was speaking he was studying the occupants of the room, his gaze cold and analytical, giving nothing away—until he saw and recognised Giselle. On her he allowed his gaze to rest just that little bit longer, so that she would be aware of his recognition of her and be forced to recognise the mistake she had made when she had stolen his parking spot.

Giselle felt the anger in his gaze scorching her conscience, but years of forcing herself never to appear outwardly vulnerable had her lifting her head and meeting his gaze head-on.

She was daring to challenge him? Saul was a recognisably formidable man, whom no one defied—especially not someone who was in the wrong, and especially not when that someone was financially dependent on him, as this woman most decidedly was. He was used to women attempting to bring themselves to his attention because they desired him and his wealth, not so that they could challenge him.

Twice now she had angered him, which meant that she now had two debts to repay—and he would see that she settled up, Saul decided as the senior partner began to introduce his junior architects to him.

Why, *why*, of all the men parking their cars in London had she had to steal the parking spot of *this* man? Giselle agonised inwardly. There was no point in telling herself that her behaviour had been out of character and born of desperation—that would not mean anything to the man slowly making his way towards her.

One by one he spoke to all the juniors, asking them which part of the plan they had worked on. Bill, of course, immediately went into his 'I'm a team player and I get everyone onside with me' routine, whilst at the same time managing to send a look in her direction which said that *she* was not part of that team. Little did Bill know that he had no need to try to make their new client have doubts about her. She'd already done a wonderful job of that herself.

Her stomach tense with apprehension, Giselle waited, and waited, knowing that retribution was going to fall, and knowing too that he was enjoying drawing out her torment.

And then he was standing in front of her, the powerful magnetic quality of his personality causing her to take a step back from him

'And you, Ms...?'

'Giselle,' Giselle answered. 'Giselle Freeman.'

'And your contribution to the plans was...?'

'Cold storage, wasn't it?' someone laughed, but Giselle ignored them.

'I worked on the air conditioning, with an ecological brief to be incorporated,' she said stiffly.

'A brief which I think I am correct in saying is currently running over-budget?' Saul pointed out as he allowed his gaze to slide slowly and thoroughly over her.

He'd picked up on the look Bill had given her and had guessed that she was as unpopular with them as she'd made herself with him. That would mean that she was not an effective team player, and that would hinder work on any project in which she participated. He was surprised that the practice kept her on.

Giselle's heart pounded with fear. She'd been transferred to work on the air conditioning because it had run over-budget and because she was known to be good at working within budget—but she could hardly say so when not even Mr Shepherd had come to her defence.

Saul Parenti was playing with her, she knew. He was going to ask for her to be removed from the project, she could tell, and then she would probably be sacked. A cold sweat began to break out on her skin, and her stomach was churning with nausea. She couldn't lose her job. She mustn't. And beneath her fear was an angry contempt for this man who was using his power to torment her that she dared not let him see.

'I am not happy with the car parking arrangements for the complex,' Saul continued, turning back to the senior partner and breaking the tense silence that had gripped the room. 'Perhaps Giselle should work on those, whilst someone with more experience takes over from her with the air conditioning.'

Giselle could feel her face burning. He had both insulted her professional ability and scored a point over her for her morning run-in with him. He had humiliated her publicly, she admitted helplessly, as the senior partner hastily assured him that, yes, indeed, she could do exactly that.

As Saul Parenti left the office with Mr Shepherd, Giselle lifted her chin. She wasn't going to let anyone, least of all him, know how hurt and afraid she felt.

She was still daring to challenge him, Saul thought furiously as he saw her lifted chin. Well, she'd soon learn that that was a dangerous mistake. Dangerous for her.

CHAPTER TWO

SEVERAL hours later, still seated in one of the senior partners' offices, whilst they thrashed out the details of the revised plans, Saul found that his thoughts were still straying irritatingly to Giselle.

It was unheard of for any woman to occupy his thoughts when they should be focused on more important matters, and turning this project from the disaster it had been heading for into a financially successful venture was important to him both on a business and a personal level. His success as an entrepreneur had brought him plenty of competitors who resented his success and would be happy to see him fail.

But he was not going to fail—as he had already been making plain to the senior partners via his caustic condemnation of the excesses proposed by the island's previous owner and what Saul considered to be the firm's lax attitude to the control and costing of the plans it had been responsible for drawing up.

'I do not have the time to sift through every detail of each part of the plan and its costing to ensure that your people are doing what I have instructed them to do,' Saul pointed out acerbically. 'And yet it is essential that they do exactly that if this project is to be successful and ultimately financially viable.'

'I accept that.' Mr Shepherd nodded.

'Good. To ensure that my wishes are carried out what I propose is that you second to me one of your best junior architects—someone who would be directly responsible to me for ensuring that the plans adhere to my requirements, and for alerting both me and you should they fail to do so.'

'That sounds an excellent idea,' the Senior Partner agreed.

'I shall require someone well qualified and able to carry out such a role,' Saul told him warningly.

'Of course—and I think I know exactly the right person. You met her earlier—Giselle Freeman.'

Saul looked sharply at the senior partner to assure himself that the other man was not attempting some kind of ridiculous joke. The last person he would want for such a role was Giselle Freeman. The older man's expression, though, was completely serious and free from humour, leaving Saul to battle with a variety of unfamiliar emotions. It was very rare for him to be caught off-guard, and even more rare for him to find that he was in a situation he did not wish to be in and could not easily get out of. Shepherd might not be joking, but Saul's suspicions were aroused that he could be trying to offload an unwanted and ineffective member of his staff off on him. He certainly wasn't going to allow *that* to happen, and thankfully—because of his suspicions— Saul could now see a way of rejecting the other man's recommendation.

'Yes. I remember. She's been working on the air

conditioning plans. I gained the impression that she isn't very popular with her colleagues. Anyone seconded to me in the role I envisage will have to be able to work well with other people.'

'There is some hostility towards Giselle in that office,' the senior partner agreed. 'But it is not her fault.' He sighed, and then continued, 'The truth is that Giselle is far better qualified than her colleagues. She graduated with honours and won an internationally acclaimed prize for her final-year project. She's a dedicated, hardworking professional with the qualifications to have a glittering career in front of her. The reality is that because of the downturn we simply don't have the work for her here that would put her skills to their best use. She's extremely loyal, though. An exemplary employee. I happen to know that in her first year here with us she was approached by two different headhunters working on behalf of international concerns. One job offer was in the Arabian Gulf, the other was in Singapore, but she chose to stay with us. She's only been working on the air con plans because the chap who was doing so before made such a complete hash of things that we had to move him on to something less demanding.'

Saul's expression had grown more grim with every word of praise the senior partner had given Giselle. Praise for her was not, after all, what he had wanted to hear—but now that he *had* heard it, and if she was as good as the senior partner was claiming, it would look decidedly odd and unbusinesslike if he refused to have her working for him. Saul was too good a businessman to allow his personal feelings to affect his business decisions. She might not appeal to him as a woman, but as an architect she was apparently very much 'best in class'. And he simply did not have time to waste sifting through a whole raft of possible candidates with potentially inferior abilities. The reality was that the project needed to get underway and be completed with some speed if he was to make the profit he wanted from it.

'Very well,' he agreed, before warning, 'but if I find she isn't up to the job then I'll expect you to take her back and supply me with someone else.'

Having dealt with the senior partner, Saul resolved grimly that if Giselle was to be seconded to work for him then there was one thing she would have to be taught—and speedily. The rules he made she would have to obey, or face the consequences.

'I imagine you will want the secondment to commence as soon as possible?' said the senior partner.

'Yes,' Saul confirmed. He suspected that Giselle Freeman would want to work for him as little as he wanted her to, and that would certainly afford him a certain amount of cynical satisfaction—that and making sure she knew just how much she had transgressed by stealing the car parking space for which he had been waiting so patiently. He already had a plan to make sure she knew that, though. He had already confirmed that the Human Resources department held copies of the keys to all the company cars, and now the spare keys to Giselle's car were in his pocket.

Not that he should be wasting his valuable mental energy on Giselle, Saul warned himself. He had far more important things to think about—one of the most pressing of which was the financial problems currently being experienced by his cousin.

Normally Saul enjoyed problem-solving. He thrived on juggling a variety of problems and then finding solutions to them. Doing just that had been his way through the bleakness of his despair in the long months after his parents' death, when he had struggled to cope with their loss.

They had been killed when a building had collapsed on them after they had gone to the aid of victims of an earthquake disaster in South America. The pain his parents' death had brought him had shocked him. Like their deaths, he hadn't been prepared for it. His overwhelming emotion initially had been anger—anger because they had risked and lost their lives, anger because they had not thought of how their deaths might affect him, anger because they had not loved him enough to ensure that they would always be there for him. It had been then that he had recognised the effect the loss of parental love and simply 'being there' could have on a child—even when that child was eighteen and officially an adult.

He had sworn then that he would never have a child himself, in case he unwittingly caused it to suffer the pain he himself was suffering. That was when he had also fully recognised just how glad he was that it was his younger cousin who was heir to the family title and lands and not him, that it was on his cousin's shoulders that the responsibility to do his duty would rest for putting their small landlocked country before his own desires.

Aldo wasn't like him. He was a quiet, gentle academic—no match for the scheming daughter of a Russian oligarch who was now his wife, and with whom he was so obviously and desperately in love. Poor fool.

Saul did not believe in love. Desire, lust, sexual hunger—yes. But allying those things to emotion and calling it love—no, never. That was not for him. He preferred his emotional freedom and the security it gave him—the knowledge that he would never again suffer the pain he had experienced when he had lost his parents.

Where Aldo thrived on tradition and continuity, Saul thrived on mastering challenges. And the Kovoca Island project was turning out to be a very considerable challenge indeed. Under-funded and over-budget, the original project had contributed to the financial downfall of the island's previous owner—who, it seemed to Saul, had wanted to outdo Dubai in his plans for the island.

Saul had already drawn a red line through his predecessor's plans for an underwater hotel, complete with a transparent underwater walkway, and for a road connecting the hotel and the island to the mainland. Just as he had drawn a red line through an equally over-ambitious plan to turn the island's single snow-capped mountain into a winter ski resort, complete with imported snow.

It was a pity that for now at least he could not draw a similar red line though Giselle Freeman's involvement in the project.

Everyone else might be celebrating the fact that the new owner of the Kovoca Island had given the go-ahead to the previous owner's project and was keeping them on as its architects, and were keen to show their commitment by working late into the evening, but Giselle had another client to deal with—which was why right now she was on her way to the car park to collect her car. She would drive over to the shabby offices of the small charity which, having been left a plot of land, was now keen to develop it into a community centre and accommodation for homeless people. The charity had appealed for architectural help with the project and Giselle had taken it on as a non-fee-paying commission, in her own free time, with the agreement of her employers that she could use their facilities.

It was important not only that the new building blended in with its surroundings and provided the facilities the charity wanted, but also that it would be affordable to build and to run, and Giselle had spent a great deal of her spare time looking into various ways of meeting all three of those targets.

Then tonight when she got home she would have to e-mail the matron of the retirement home in which her great-aunt lived to see if her aunt had recovered from her cold yet.

Meadowside was an excellent facility, and its elderly residents were really well cared for, but it was also extremely expensive. The invested money from the sale of Great-Aunt Maude's house paid half the monthly fees and Giselle paid the other half. It was the least she could do, given what her great aunt had done for her—taking her in, looking after her and loving her despite everything that had happened.

Giselle felt her stomach muscles starting to tense. It was always like this whenever she was forced to think about the past. She knew that she would never be able to forget what had happened. Even now if the squeal of car tyres caught her unawares the sound had the power to make her freeze into immobile panic. The memories, the images were always there—the wet road, the darkness, her mother telling her to hold on to the pram containing her baby brother as they turned to cross the road. But she hadn't held on to the pram. She had let go. She was starting to breathe too shallowly and too fast, her heart pounding sickly. The sounds—screams, screeching tyres, breaking glass—the spin of the pram's wheels as it lay there in the road, the smells—petrol, rain, blood.

No!

As always, the denial inside her was silent, as she had been silent, digging her nails into the palm of her hand. The hand that should have been gripping the pram handle—the hand which she had pulled away, defying her mother's screamed demand that she stayed where she was, holding onto the pram.

Giselle could see her mother's face now, and hear her screamed command; she could see her fear, and could see too the sleeping face of her baby brother where he'd lain in the pram just before it had left the pavement, straight in the path of an oncoming lorry.

It was over...over... There was no bringing back the dead. But it could never really be over—not for her. But at least no one else apart from her great-aunt knew what she knew.

Initially after the deaths of her mother and baby brother Giselle had continued to live with her father, an overworked GP, with a kind neighbour taking and collecting her from school along with her own children. That time had been the darkest of Giselle's life. Her father, overwhelmed by his own grief, had shut her out, excluding her, not wanting her around—as she had always felt—because she'd reminded him of what he had lost. His emotional distance from her had increased her guilt and her own misery.

And then her great-aunt had come to visit, and it had been arranged that when she returned home Giselle would go with her. She had longed for her father to insist that he wanted her to stay, just as she had longed for him to hold her and tell her that he loved her, that he didn't blame her. But he hadn't. She could see his face now— the last time she had seen it—as he'd nodded his head in agreement with her great-aunt's suggestions, gaunt and drawn, his gaze avoiding her. He had died less than six months afterwards from a fatal heart attack.

As a child Giselle had felt that he had chosen to die to be with her mother and brother rather than live and be with her. Even now sometimes, in her darkest and most despairing moments, she still thought that. If he'd loved her, he'd have kept her with him... But he hadn't.

Not that she'd been unhappy with her great-aunt. She hadn't. Her great-aunt had loved and cared for her, building a new life for her. Of course it had helped that her great-aunt had lived nearly a hundred miles away from the home Giselle had shared with her parents and her baby brother.

Giselle started to walk faster, as though to escape from her own painful memories. Even now, after nearly twenty years, she couldn't bear to think about what had happened. Her great-aunt had been wonderfully kind and generous in taking her in, and Giselle wanted to do everything she could to make sure the now very elderly lady was well looked after. Without her job it would of course be impossible for her to find the money needed to keep her aunt in her excellent retirement home. And

that meant that, no matter how much she might personally resent Saul Parenti and his attitude towards her, she
had to be grateful for the fact that he was continuing
with the project and keeping the firm on. These were
hard times, and to lose such a valuable source of income
would have meant redundancies.

Giselle had never imagined when she had been studying and working so hard for her qualifications that there
would be such a deep downturn in the economy—one
that would affect the construction industry so badly. She
had chosen architecture as her career in part because she
had believed that she would always be able to find work.
Work—and getting paid for it—were vitally important
to a woman who had already made up her mind that
she would have to provide for herself financially all her
life, because she was determined never to share her life
with a partner. And in part she had chosen it because
she had fallen in love with buildings—great houses and
other buildings owned by the National Trust which her
great-aunt had taken her to visit so often whilst she had
been growing up.

Engaged in her own thoughts, Giselle headed automatically for her parked car, but as she approached the
bay instead of seeing her own car all she could see was
the highly polished bonnet of a much larger vehicle in
the space where hers should have been. Automatically
her walking pace slowed, and then she stopped as she
looked round, wondering if she had been mistaken about
where she had parked. The click of a car door opening
caught her attention. She turned in the direction of the
sound, her heart plummeting as she saw Saul Parenti
getting out of the car with the long bonnet, the one that

was parked where she'd expected to see her own car, and coming towards her.

Her reaction was immediate—a gut-deep instinct that went beyond logic or reason, making her confront him and demand, before she could think about the reckless-ness of doing so, 'Where is my car? What have you done with it?'

For sheer blind arrogance he doubted she had any equal, Saul decided, listening to her and witnessing her immediate hostility.

Her response confirmed every judgement he had already made about her, and reinforced his growing determination to put her in her place.

'I had it removed from my parking space,' he told her meaningfully.

'Removed?' Giselle felt the file she was holding slip from her grasp as the shock hit her, disgorging papers as it fell. 'Removed?' she repeated 'How? Where to?'

She knew her voice was trembling under the weight of her shocked emotions, but as she dropped to her haunches to pick up the contents of her file she was helpless to control it. She hated the effect this man seemed to have on her. She had hated it from their first confrontation and she hated it even more now. It made her feel vulnerable and afraid—it made her behave with a defensive antagonism she couldn't control. It made her want to turn and run away from him. But most of all it made her so acutely aware of him as a man that she hardly dared even breathe, for fear he would somehow sense how physically aware of him her body was. It wasn't just the shameful stiffening of her nipples, nor even the shockingly purposeful beat of the gnawing pulse aching through her lower body. No, it was the feeling that a whole protective layer had been ripped from every inch of her skin, leaving it so sensitive and reactive to his physical presence that it was as though he had already touched her so intimately that her body knew him—and still wanted him.

How had this happened to her? Giselle didn't know. It must be because of Saul himself—because of the intense aura of male sexuality he gave off. No other man had ever affected her like this. It shocked her that she could be so vulnerable so quickly to a man she didn't know and didn't think she'd like if she did know him. She'd controlled her emotions and her desires for so long that she'd believed she was safe. She must have let her guard slip somehow without realising it. But she could make things right again. She could make herself safe. All she had to do was keep away from Saul Parenti—and that should be easy enough. At least he didn't want her. That would have been dreadful. She should be grateful for the fact that he was so obviously furious with her.

'How?' he was repeating tauntingly. 'How are illegally parked cars normally removed? And as to where...'

She'd stepped back from him, giving him a haughty look that suggested his proximity was something she wanted to reject, Saul recognised, and his male pride was now as antagonised by her attitude as his temper. Women did not step back from him. Quite the opposite. They clung to him—sometimes far more than he wanted them to do.

Just for a moment Saul mentally allowed himself the pleasure of picturing Giselle clinging to him, her face turned up beseechingly towards his own. That would be a *pleasure?* Having her want him to bed her? Was he going mad? There was nothing about her that aroused him sexually, nothing at all. He liked his women softly feminine, not challenging and aggressive. He liked them warm and welcoming, not icy cold and rejecting. The thought of taming such a shrew might excite some men, but he was not one of them.

Having stepped back from Saul to what she hoped was a safe distance from the lure of his sexuality, Giselle managed to drag together the determination to insist, 'My car was not parked illegally, and if you've had it clamped and towed away then *you* are the one who is breaking the law.'

Oh, yes, she was definitely a shrew, Saul decided as he bent to retrieve a stray sheet of paper that had fluttered close to his feet. Automatically he scanned the print on it and then paused to read it more slowly before demanding, 'You're working on this project free of charge?'

Desperate to retrieve the paper, Giselle reached for it, almost snatching it from him in her fear of accidentally coming into physical contact with him.

'And what if I am?' she defended herself sharply. 'It doesn't have anything to do with you, and you have no right to question me.'

There she went again, challenging him with her open animosity to him, when by rights she ought to be humbling herself, admitting her previous fault and seeking his forgiveness.

He had, Saul decided, had enough.

The history of his genes meant that he was not a man who allowed anyone to challenge him, and for a challenge to go unanswered was unthinkable. He might not rule Arezzio, but his ancestors had. They had ruled it and held it against all those who had challenged their right to it. Their blood flowed in his veins and those who defied him—in any way—did so at their own risk.

'You think not?'

The silky tone of his voice had an electrifying effect on her, causing the fine hairs at the nape of her neck to stand on end, her flesh to react as though he had touched it, caressed it.

'I understand from Mr Shepherd at the practice that your job is very important to you?'

'He told you that?' The words were spoken before Giselle could hold them back. She shivered inwardly with apprehension, unable to conceal the shocked fear that darkened her green eyes to a deep jade. She hadn't realised that Mr Shepherd even knew how much her job security mattered to her, never mind discussing it with someone else.

So he had found something that made her feel vulnerable. Saul applauded himself.

'He said that you had turned down far more prestigious job offers and career opportunities to remain with the firm—something which he appears to consider a mark of employee loyalty. I, on the other hand, believe your motivation must be something far more powerful, and am curious to know just what it is.'

He was curious about her? Even as he had spoken the words Saul had felt the jolt of wariness that had shocked through him.

What was it about this woman that was having such an unprecedented effect on him? First she antagonised him and aroused his anger. Now she was arousing his curiosity. Deep within him a normally silent voice was asking him the unthinkable. If she could touch the emotions he normally controlled so tightly that they were immune to being touched, and if he allowed himself to be aroused physically by her, then what would happen? Did he really need to ask? He knew, after all, what happened when someone put a light to a keg of dynamite. The result was destruction. *Destruction?* Did this infuriating woman have the power to arouse him to the point where that arousal could destroy the barriers he had put in place to keep him immune to the weakness of needing one specific other person in his life? Impossible, Saul reassured himself.

Saul was waiting for her response, Giselle knew—just as she knew that she didn't want to answer him.

'Why stay in a job for which you are over-qualified and I daresay underpaid? Unless, of course, you fear that all those qualifications of yours are merely pieces of paper and that in reality you are not up to the work you would be required to do at a higher level.'

Saul pressed her, determined not to step back from his probing just because of an inner warning he refused to give credence to.

His accusation jolted Giselle into an immediate repudiation.

'Of course I'm up to it.' Angry pride reflected in both Giselle's voice and the look she gave him. 'And I am confident that I could do any job I was offered.'

'Are you now?' Her assertion showed him yet another strand to her personality. With the revelation of each new strand he felt increasingly compelled to know more about her. Because she infuriated and antagonised him. Because she was so unlike any other woman he knew. Because she didn't treat him as they did, with delight and docility, eager to please him and pleasure him, his own inner voice dryly mocked him.

She was obviously determined not to answer him, but Saul was equally determined that he would have an answer. He changed tack, saying silkily, 'Correct me if I am wrong, but the Kovoca Island project is, as I understand it, all that currently stands between your employers and insolvency—and with that insolvency the loss of your job?'

Giselle's mouth went dry and her heart started pounding wretchedly heavily as she recognised the threat in his words. She was forced to concede. 'Yes, that is correct.'

'Given your employer has suggested to me that it will facilitate matters if you are seconded to me, to ensure that in future all redrawn plans and costings are in line with my requirements, I should have thought that it is only natural that I would have the right to enquire into your reliability and your probity—in all professional matters.'

Silenced by the shock of what she had just learned, Giselle could only stare at him in appalled dismay.

This couldn't be happening. He—her tormentor— could not be standing there saying that she would be working directly with him, that she would in effect be responsible to him and thus in his power. But he was, Giselle acknowledged as she fought against the panic washing through her at full flood force. If only she could tell him to find someone else to be seconded to him.

If only she could turn on her heel and walk away from him…if only he didn't affect her in the way that he did. So many if onlys. Her life was full of them—heart-sickening, cruelly destructive words that spoke of what could never be. She was trapped, by duty and by love, and she had to hold on to this job even though that now meant that she would be in Saul's power.

At least he did not know how vulnerable she was to him as a woman, Giselle tried to comfort herself. A man like him must be so used to arousing desire in her sex that he simply took it for granted—just as he seemed to take his pick of the beautiful women who flocked around him, from what Emma had told her. Well, he'd certainly never want to pick her. Thank goodness.

'It is not my choice that you be my point person on this project,' Saul pointed out. 'And given what I already know about your inclination towards theft I must warn you that you will be very much on probation. The first sign I see that you are using the same unscrupulous methods you used to gain access to my parking space in your work, you will be out of a job.'

'I made a mistake—' Giselle tried to defend herself, but Saul wasn't in any mood to be compassionate.

'A very big mistake,' he agreed. 'And you will be making another if you don't show some honesty now and tell me why you turned down two prestigious jobs. I won't have someone whose morals I find suspect working for me in a position of trust.'

His meaning was perfectly plain, and it caused Giselle to blench.

Watching her, Saul felt confident that now she would tell him what he could do with his job. That was certainly what he wanted her to do. Loath as he was to admit it, somehow or other she had got under his skin in a way that he was finding increasingly hard to ignore—like an annoying, irritating, unignorable itch that needed to be scratched. He didn't want that kind of intrusion in his life.

Giselle was trying not to let Saul see how vulnerable and anxious she felt. He wanted her to hand in her notice, she suspected. But she was not going to do so. She couldn't.

His accusations might be unjust, and she might feel angry, but anger was a luxury that she couldn't afford, Giselle was forced to concede.

She took a deep breath and said, as calmly as she could, 'Very well. I will tell you.'

Her response was not what Saul had been expecting—and very definitely not what he had wanted.

Lifting her head, Giselle continued, 'I turned down the other jobs because the great-aunt who brought me up now needs full-time care, and in addition to helping fund that I want to be here to ensure that the care is as good as the care she gave me. I can't expect her to leave Yorkshire after she's spent her whole life there, but I do expect myself to be here for her, doing everything I can to ensure that she has all the comfort and care she deserves. Working in London means that I can see her regularly. If I worked abroad that wouldn't be possible.'

Against all his own expectations Saul felt an unwilling tug of grudging respect—and something more.

'You were brought up by your great-aunt? What

happened to your parents?' he felt impelled to ask, the words almost dragged from him against his will.

'They died, and I was orphaned,' Giselle answered as steadily as she could, proud of how calm she managed to keep her voice.

Damn, *damn*. Saul swore inwardly as the result of his forcefulness was made plain to him along with something else—something that touched the deepest part of him, no matter how much he might wish that it did not. That single word 'orphaned' had such resonance for him—such personal and deep-rooted private emotional history.

He might have forced a confession from Giselle Freeman, but he wasn't going to be able to force a resignation from her, given what she had just told him.

He started to turn away from her, and then something stopped him. 'How old were you when…when you lost your parents?'

His voice was low, the words betraying something which in another man Giselle might almost have thought was a hushed, respectful hesitancy. But this man would never show that kind of compassion to anyone, Giselle was sure—much less someone he disliked as much as he had made it plain he disliked her.

'Seven.' Well, nearly seven. But there hadn't been a party to celebrate her November birthday that year—just as there hadn't been the year before either. A picture slid remorselessly into her head: coffins, two of them, one for her mother and one for the baby brother who had been buried with her, his coffin heaped with white flowers. And the house she had returned to with her father, filled with the agonising silence of his grief and her own guilt. She had longed so much for her father to hold her and tell her that it wasn't her fault, but instead he had turned away from her, and she'd known he did blame her, just as she blamed herself. They had never talked about what had happened. Instead he had let her great-aunt take her away because he couldn't bear the sight of her.

Seven! A thought, a fleeting memory of himself at that age, hazy and shadowed: his mother laughing as she stroked a smear of dirt from his cheek, how as that child he had felt his love for her and his happiness because she was there spill out of him to mix with the sunshine.

Saul felt the sour taste of his own revulsion against whatever it was that allowed children to be deprived of the love of their parents. He had been eighteen and he had found it hard enough to cope, even though by then he had thought himself independent and adult.

More memories were surging through the barriers Giselle wanted to put up against them. The other children at the new school she had gone to when her great-aunt had taken her in, feeling sorry for her because she didn't have parents. They had meant to be kind, of course, but then they hadn't known the truth.

In her desperation to close the door on those memories, Giselle made a small agonised sound of protest. She wished desperately that her car was here. If it had been she could have stepped past him and got into it and escaped, putting an end to her present humiliation.

Saul, hearing that sound and recognising the pain it contained—a pain he himself had felt and knew—heard himself saying before he could stop himself, 'I lost my parents when I was eighteen. You think at that age that everyone is immortal.'

Silently they looked at one another.

What was he doing? Saul derided himself. This wasn't the sort of conversation he had with anyone, never mind a woman who rubbed him up the wrong way and whom he'd already decided he didn't particularly like. It had been that word *orphaned* that had done it. Seven years old and taken in by a great-aunt she now had to help support. That explained the cheap suit, Saul reflected.

She'd implied that there wasn't currently a man in her life, but she must have had lovers. She might not be his type, but he'd be lying to himself if he didn't admit that physically she had the kind of looks that turned male heads, and that mix of stitched-up coldness allied to the suppressed passion that flashed in her eyes when she couldn't quite control it would have plenty of members of his sex keen to pursue her.

Fire and ice—that was what she was. How many lovers had she had? he wondered, the question sneaking up on him before he could stop it. Two? Three? Certainly no more than could be counted on the fingers of one hand, he suspected. What was he thinking? Whatever it was he must stop now—must not allow it to get hold and take root.

'What happened to your parents? Mine died carrying out aid work at the site of an earthquake, when a huge aftershock destroyed the building they were in.'

Giselle's muscles clenched—both against what he was saying and against the shock of his question.

'After my parents' death I wanted to talk about it, but

no one would let me. I suppose they thought it would be too…' he stopped.

'Too painful for you.' Giselle supplied, her voice cracking slightly, like an unhealed scab over a still raw wound.

What had been a hostile confrontation between them had somehow or other veered sharply into something else and somewhere else—a territory that was both familiar to her and yet at the same time unexplored by her. Because she was too afraid? Because it hurt too much?

She spoke slowly at first, the effort of speaking about something so deeply traumatic and personal making her throat feel raw.

'My mother and…and my baby brother were killed in a road accident. My father died from a heart attack eleven months after the accident.'

'I'm sorry.' He was, Saul recognised. Sorry for the child she had been, sorry for her loss, sorry he had asked now that he knew the full extent of the tragedy.

'Life is so fragile,' Giselle heard herself telling him. 'My baby brother was only six months old.' She shuddered. "I can't imagine how parents must feel when they lose a child—especially one so young—or how they cope with the responsibility of protecting such vulnerability. I'd never have a second's peace. I could never…I would never want that responsibility.'

There was a finality in her words that found an echo within him.

She had said too much, revealed and betrayed too much, Giselle recognised. Not that she had told him everything. She would never and could never tell anyone everything. Some things were so painful, so shocking and so dark that they could never be shared—had to be kept hidden away from everyone. She could just imagine how people would treat her if they knew the truth, how suspicious of her they would be—and with good reason. No, she could never speak openly about her guilt or her fear. They were burdens she must carry alone.

But she must not dwell on the past, but instead live in the present, with her duty to her great-aunt. Determinedly she focused her thoughts on the issue that had led to this unexpected and far too intimate conversation, telling Saul, 'If you want to cancel the secondment now that you have the answer to your question…'

She wanted him to cancel the secondment, Saul recognised, ignoring the fact that he had wanted to cancel it himself as he let his male drive to win take over.

'You wouldn't have been my choice. However, I don't have the time to interview other applicants. Of course if you want to withdraw…' He let the offer hang there.

'You already know that I can't,' Giselle said stiffly.

Saul shrugged.

'I doubt that either of us is happy with the situation, but for different reasons it seems that we shall have to endure it and make the best of it.'

Giselle exhaled. Talking about her past had drained her emotionally and physically, and now she felt dreadfully weak and shaky—but there was still something she needed to know.

'My car—' she began, and then stopped when she realised how thin and thready her voice sounded. She was perilously close to the limits of her self-control, she knew. Her head was beginning to ache from the stress of their confrontation. Her lips felt dry. She moistened them with the tip of her tongue.

Saul watched the telltale movement of her tongue-tip, his gaze sliding unwillingly down to the small movement of her throat as she swallowed. Her upswept hair revealed the length of her neck and the neat shape of her ears. Mauve shadows lay beneath her eyes like small bruises; her face was drained of any other colour. Something inside him ached and twisted, an emotion he didn't recognise giving birth to an impulse to reach out and touch her, hold her.

Hold her? Why?

Why? He was a man, wasn't he? And the way she had just drawn attention to her own mouth had had its obvious effect on his body. That was why he felt impelled to touch her. Right now, if he leaned forward and pressed his thumb to that special place behind her ear, if he stroked his fingertips the length of her throat, if he ran his tongue over the soft pillows of flesh that were her lips, he could make her pale skin flush softly with the warmth of arousal. He could make the pulse beat in her throat with desire for him. He could make those green eyes darken to jade and the breath shudder from her lungs. Saul took a step towards her.

Immediately Giselle stepped back from him, with a gasp of sound that brought him back to reality. What the hell was the matter with him? Saul castigated himself. The last thing he felt for her was desire, and the second last thing he wanted was her desire for him. Stepping back from her, he reached for his mobile and spoke into it, announcing, 'You can bring the car back now.'

Less than five minutes later Giselle watched as her

car was driven into the car park towards her. A uniformed driver got out and handed over the keys to Saul before heading for Saul's own gleaming car.

Without a word Giselle got into her car. She had no idea how they had acquired keys for it, and she wasn't going to ask. She was beginning to suspect that for a man like Saul Parenti anything and everything was achievable.

Saul watched her drive away. Fire and ice—a dangerous combination, designed to tempt the strongest-willed man when combined in a woman. He, though, could and would resist that temptation.

CHAPTER THREE

IT WAS nearly two weeks now since Giselle had begun her new duties in the impressive modern office building that was the headquarters of Saul Parenti's business empire, and of course she wasn't in the least bit disappointed that not once during those two very busy weeks had she seen Saul himself and that the glass-fronted office his PA had pointed out to her as his had remained empty. Far from it. She was delighted that he wasn't in evidence, and that she had been able to take up her new role without having to contend with his presence.

Or at least she had been until something had come to light this morning, whilst she had been checking over the latest batch of reworked plans couriered over to her.

Was what she had picked up a simple mistake? Was it a trick to try and catch her out, instituted by Saul himself? Or was it—and her stomach tensed at the thought of this—a deliberate attempt to defraud the Parenti Organisation, put in place by one of her own colleagues?

Whichever of the three options she chose to believe, the initial outcome was the same, and that was that she would have to report what she had seen to Saul Parenti.

Giselle looked towards the office of Saul's PA, Moira Wilson, wondering if she should discuss her concern with her.

She liked the older woman, who had gone out of her way to make her feel at home in her new environment. On her first morning here, Moira had gone through everything with her, informing her with a smile, 'I'll just run through a few things with you. First, we are all on first-name terms here—Saul insists on it. But don't mistake that for a lack of discipline or respect. He demands and gets both. I've got some forms here from HR for you to fill in—personal details, that kind of thing. Whilst you're here your salary will be increased in accordance with the levels Saul pays those who work for him, and you will be eligible for an annual bonus, medical insurance, and a car allowance. Any expenses you incur in the course of your work should be submitted to the accounts department on a monthly basis, and I should warn you that here we do not have a culture of fudging such expenses—if you take my meaning.'

This last piece of information had been accompanied by a grim look which had ensured that Giselle knew exactly what she meant.

'I never fudge my expenses. It would go against my principles to do so,' Giselle had responded truthfully.

'Excellent. I am sure you will fit in very well here,' had been Moira's response, before she had added, 'Oh, and when you complete your personal details form I shall need your passport details.'

'My passport?'

'Yes. You do have one, don't you? If not we must sort one out for you, just in case you are required to travel abroad on behalf of the company with Saul—to site meetings and that kind of thing. Saul takes a very personal and keen interest in all his projects, and is very hands-on about checking their progress.'

'Yes,' she had a passport, Giselle had confirmed. She was also used to travelling abroad to conferences and site meetings with clients—so why on earth had that tingle of something she refused to name zipped down her spine? It was doing so now, at the memory—as though someone had feathered a touch against her bare skin. What was happening to her? Nothing, Giselle assured herself fiercely. Nothing was happening to her and nothing was going to happen to her. Normally she enjoyed visiting the various sites she worked on, especially when they were abroad. It made up for the fact that she had missed out on the kind of foreign trips enjoyed by most of her peers when they had been growing up.

Her great-aunt simply hadn't had the money for that kind of luxury. Additionally, the circumstances of her life—the dreadful tragedy that still haunted her and filled her with guilt—meant that she had always been wary of allowing others to get close to her even as friends, so she hadn't joined in the group holidays abroad enjoyed by her peers during her early twenties, even when she could have financed them herself. Instead she had concentrated on getting the very best qualifications she could. Then, when she had started to think about taking solo holidays to explore the architecture of other countries, her great-aunt had needed to move into residential care, and once again there simply hadn't been the money for such unnecessary expenses.

Giselle judged Moira to be somewhere in her early

fifties, which had surprised her. From Emma's com-ments about Saul's lifestyle she had imagined that his PA would be glamorous and nubile, not a woman of Moira's age, even if she was a very smart and elegant fifty-something. Her appearance was much like that of the other women Giselle had seen in the offices, making her acutely conscious of the shabbiness of her own clothes. There was nothing she could do about that, though. Only two days ago she had received a letter informing her that regrettably the fees for her great-aunt's care and accom-modation were to be increased by twenty per cent—not far short of the unexpected increase in her salary. There were cheaper care homes, but Giselle was determined that her great-aunt would go on enjoying the level of comfort she had where she was—even if that did mean she herself would have to go without the new clothes she had been tempted to buy, having seen how smart the other women working here were.

Now, as she looked round her spacious office, Giselle admitted that in many ways she preferred her new work-ing environment—even if she would rather have worked for the devil himself than Saul Parenti. She doubted that she would be missed by her old colleagues. The men she worked with had shown quite plainly prior to her departure that they resented the fact that she had been selected over them for what they considered to be a prestigious and career-boosting opportunity, and of course her own pride had not allowed her to tell them that she would have preferred not to be chosen. However, it was the well-meaning Emma's words that were still sending scalding waves of humiliation burning painfully through Giselle's emotions.

She had spoken to her in private. 'It's just as well that it's you who's been seconded to go and work for Saul Parenti. If it was anyone else then all the other girls would be seething with jealousy at the thought of someone getting the opportunity to work closely with such a fabulously sexy man. But of course they won't be jealous of you, because they all know that there's no danger of you attracting him—not with your attitude to men and the way you give them the cold shoulder. Especially not with a man like Saul, who can have any woman he wants.'

Giselle knew it was ridiculous of her to feel humiliated by Emma's remarks—somehow less of a woman. After all, Giselle herself had always made it plain that she wasn't interested in flirting with or attracting men, cold-shouldering their advances and retreating into herself whenever they showed any interest in her. The last thing she wanted was a man pursuing her—any man—and especially a man like Saul Parenti. Why especially him? Because she was afraid that she might be vulnerable to him? Because she was afraid that she might actually want him?

Giselle stood up, panicked by her own thoughts, and then subsided back into her chair. Of course not. It was nothing to do with anything like that. She knew that she was perfectly safe from desiring Saul Parenti, and even if by some foolish misjudgement she did, she also knew that it was impossible for anything to come of that desire. Because, as Emma had made clear, Saul Parenti would never find her desirable? No! Because she did not *want* him to desire her—just as she did not want *any* man to desire her.

She had taken refuge in angry disdain, demanding of Emma, 'Does everything have to come down to sex?'

Emma had laughed and told her, 'For most of us—yes.' Before adding, 'Men can't help being men, and they are predatory by instinct. It's in their genes. But in your case… Well, what I'm trying to say, Giselle, is that…'

'That a man like Saul Parenti wouldn't find me desirable enough to want to go to the trouble of trying to seduce me?' Giselle had supplied for her colleague.

'Well, you do send a keep-your-distance vibe to men, you must admit, and men like Saul Parenti have plenty of women all too ready to give them what they want to be bothered with a woman who freezes them off. I haven't hurt your feelings, have I?' Emma had asked anxiously.

Giselle had shaken her head.

'No, of course not.' Giselle had assured her. And that was the truth. Of course she wasn't hurt because Emma had spoken the truth and said that Saul wouldn't be interested in her. She didn't want him to be. She didn't want *any* man to be interested in her. She couldn't afford to allow any man to become interested in her because she knew that she could not and must not become interested in them. She could never have in her life the relationships that others took for granted. She could not fall in love. She could not commit to anyone, and most of all she could not within that commitment help to create a child. She must never have a child. Never.

Anyway, how she looked and whether Saul Parenti did or did not see her as attractive were not subjects she should be paying any mind to. Instead she must focus on the reason she was here and on what she was being paid to do.

The office provided for her was well planned out and perfect for her duties, with its large windows flooding the room with natural light. It contained all the equipment she might need, including a good-sized table in the middle of the floor on which she was able to spread out paper copies of architectural drawings and plans—just as she had done earlier, with the new drawings and costings that had been sent over.

Uncertainly Giselle looked back at them. She had been worrying about them for so long, going back to check and then recheck them just in case she had made a mistake, that she hadn't realised how late it was. Scanning the office, she saw nearly everyone else had gone home. Moira had gone too, no doubt, without Giselle having taken the opportunity to speak with her and seek her advice.

The anomaly was definitely there. The non-frostproof terracotta tiles for the summerhouse and the area surrounding it, leading to the first of the staggered-level swimming pools, had been changed as Saul had instructed. But the tiles used in substitution were considerably more expensive, and from a supplier whose name Giselle could not remember having seen on their approved lists. As a precaution she had e-mailed a couple of approved suppliers, and they had both come back with costings far lower than the one quoted—which meant that either by accident or design the person responsible for the changed plans and materials was recommending a purchase that would cost far far more than it needed to. To make matters worse, the tiles recommended had a non-standard raised pattern, which meant that in future, should any one of them need replacing, they would have to be specially produced at a very high cost. And, worst of all by far, the person responsible for the recommendation and costing was her male colleague and adversary Bill Jeffries.

She'd e-mailed him to check discreetly with him that there hadn't been an error but it appeared that he was on leave for a week, and with Saul due back from his overseas trip in the morning there was no way Giselle could hold the plans and costings back from him until Bill Jeffries returned to the office.

She needed someone else's input and advice, she decided, making up her mind. Through the plate glass that fronted all the mezzanine offices she was delighted to spot Moira, putting on her suit jacket and preparing to leave. It had been a warm day for mid-April, with the sun streaming in through the windows, and Giselle had removed her own jacket to work more easily. She looked hesitantly at it, and then, seeing Moira heading for the door, scooped up the papers from the desk instead and hurried to intercept her.

'From what you've told me, I rather think this is something you need to discuss with Saul,' Moira judged firmly, once Giselle had reached the end of her story.

'I know he isn't due back until tomorrow, and I expect he'll have a full diary. Perhaps you...?' Giselle began, only to have Moira shake her head.

'He's actually just arrived and he's in his office,' she told her. 'Why don't you go and have a word with him now?'

Giselle's heart sank. This wasn't what she had expected or wanted to hear.

Witnessing her hesitation and reluctance, Saul's PA insisted, 'I really do think you should, Giselle. This sounds like a potentially serious matter to me, and Saul won't thank you for delaying informing him about it.' Moira looked at her watch. 'I'm sorry—I must run. I've promised to take the notes for a committee meeting of our Gardening Club this evening, and I mustn't be late. But I know Saul's planning to work late, and I can assure you that he will want to know what you've just told me. That's why you're here after all.'

It was too late now to wish that she'd kept quiet and not sought Moira's advice. Taking a deep breath, Giselle headed towards Saul's office.

Like the other offices on the mezzanine floor, Saul's was fronted by plate glass 'walls'. It might be larger than the other offices, and it might have a private inner sanctum, but that apart it was no more prestigiously furnished than her own office, Giselle noted, and it was equipped as a practical working office. Apparently for business meetings Saul used the hospitality suite on the top floor of the building.

Since Saul operated an 'open door' working policy, Giselle only knocked briefly on the glass door, which was in any event half open, before stepping into Saul's office. The brilliance of the late-afternoon sun shone into the room, momentarily blinding her, so that she didn't realise until her vision cleared that Saul wasn't there—despite the fact that his laptop was open on his desk and his suit jacket was hanging from the back of his chair. Why was it that only a certain type of very male European man seemed able to wear that particular shade of light tan successfully, whilst looking as though they could have stepped out of an Armani ad? Giselle found herself wondering distractedly. She tried very hard not to picture Saul in just that role—only to be betrayed by her traitorous imagination which suddenly, out of nowhere, managed to create an all too realistic image of Saul standing in for one of the designer's male underwear models.

Battling with her own imagination, Giselle almost dropped the papers she was hugging to her when the door connecting Saul's inner office with the outer one suddenly opened, and Saul himself stepped through it.

His easy words—'Moira, if you could manage to rustle up some coffee and a sandwich whilst I have a shower I'll be eternally grateful to you…'—changed to an abrupt and far less welcoming, 'Oh, it's you,' when he realised that it was Giselle who was standing in his office and not his PA.

It wasn't his abrupt manner that was driving hot, self-conscious colour up under her skin, though. Giselle knew that as she struggled to retain her equilibrium under the increased pounding of her heart when she realised that when he had initially come into the room Saul had been starting to unfasten his shirt. The cuffs were already loose, revealing the sinewy dark-hair-covered flesh of one arm as he reached up to push his hand into his hair in a gesture of irritation. His tie was missing and the top buttons of his shirt were unfastened, so that she could see the fine criss-crossing of the beginnings of his body hair. The rush of female awareness that flooded through her almost knocked her off balance with an alien, almost frightening power. She wasn't used to feeling like this, and the fact that she was doing so affronted and angered her, causing her to clutch the papers even more tightly to her body.

The crackle they made focused Saul's attention on her. She was breathing too fast, her lips parted, her hands trembling slightly as she gripped some papers in front of her. Her pose was almost that of an ancient civilisation virgin slave, facing the master who had bought her for his pleasure—and with it her own.

The direction his thoughts were taking didn't please Saul one little bit. He'd spent the last ten days engaged in hard negotiation to secure the prime Chinese sites he wanted for his expanding hotel chain—hard negotiation and also what had seemed at the time easy refusal of sexual favours from the socialites his hosts had introduced him to. Perhaps his body hadn't been as on-message with that refusal as he had believed, he decided grimly as he attempted to banish the images his mind was now busy conjuring up—images of a green-eyed, blonde-haired beauty wearing next to nothing, offering him the welcome and the pleasure battle-scarred warriors like his own ancestors had expected to receive as a matter of course. He, on the other hand, whilst returning triumphant from his own battle, couldn't get so much as a drink and a sandwich, and was being confronted by the abrasive secondee he had no wish to have in his life.

Giselle's voice cut across his thoughts. 'I can come back tomorrow if you're too busy to see me now.'

'I'm leaving for New York tomorrow. If it's urgent

enough for you to come and see me now, then you'd better tell me whatever it is that's brought you here. Sit down,' he commanded, before speaking into the intercom. 'Charlie, would you mind getting me a double espresso and a sandwich from across the road? Put it on my tab. I'll be in my office.'

Charlie was the doorman, as Giselle knew.

'Right,' he said to Giselle when he had finished. 'What's the problem?'

'I'm a bit concerned about a costing on one of the new plans,' Giselle answered. 'I've got the paperwork here.'

Saul made an exasperated sound.

'I can't see it whilst you're clutching it like that, can I? Bring it here and put it on the desk.'

A shaft of sunlight penetrating the shadows around his desk gave the cheap white tee shirt she was wearing an opacity that drew Saul's gaze automatically to her breasts as she dropped the papers on his desk. Her actions dragged the thin fabric against her body, so that her nipples were outlined in erotically sharp relief. His gaze lingered where the shaft of light was probing the cheap fabric, as though it possessed a male need to strip back the covering from her flesh and explore the sensuality beneath.

She must focus on why she was here and forget about the way her proximity to Saul Parenti was making her feel, Giselle told herself. But how could she when she could almost *feel* Saul's critical gaze, underlining Emma's comments about her?

The arrival of the doorman with Saul's coffee and sandwich was a welcome relief, allowing her to straighten the papers and then step back from the desk whilst Saul thanked Charlie, rewarding him with a warm smile and a few words of male banter about the doorman's favourite football team. So there was a human side to Saul Parenti—even if she was never likely to see much of it. Giselle had no idea why that should bring her such a sense of loss and exclusion. She didn't *want* him to be nice to her. Not one little bit.

'So what exactly is the problem?' Saul demanded, sitting back in his chair and drinking his coffee.

'It's this reworked plan, here,' Giselle told him. She had to lean across the desk to point out the part of the plan in question, too intent on getting the ordeal of what she had to say over and done with to be aware of the way in which her pose had brought her breasts in line with Saul's gaze.

Saul was, though. And so was his body. And it was reacting very specifically indeed to those soft teardrop-shaped curves with their tip-tilted nipples. He eased his chair closer to the desk, to conceal the giveaway tightening of his trousers as his erection swelled demandingly against the fabric. His hunger for the sandwich the doorman had brought him had suddenly been replaced by a very different and even more insistent kind of hunger.

'And your conclusion?' Saul interrupted Giselle curtly. He needed to get her out of his office and get his body back under control—and the sooner the better.

Giselle's face burned. It was obvious that Saul didn't want to listen to her and thought that she was wasting his time.

'There are three possibilities,' she answered crisply, straightening up and stepping back from the desk. 'One:

the person who drew up the plan and its costing made an error. Two: they knew what they were doing and this is a deliberate attempt to defraud your company...'

'And three?' Saul queried, recognising now that she had moved back from him that she had spotted something that could be very serious indeed. He was in no mood to thank her, though. Not whilst his body's reaction to her was so intense and unwanted.

'Three: you are deliberately testing me by setting up an error to see what I will do.'

Saul stared at her, anger driving out his desire to get rid of her.

'Let me get this straight. Are you actually suggesting that I would stoop to that kind of game-playing?'

Giselle lifted her head

'Why not? You had my car moved.'

Saul came out from behind his desk and walked towards her. Immediately Giselle took a step back from him. She could smell the hot male scent of him and it was making her dizzy, weak, igniting a low, dull, pulsing ache that was taking over her whole body.

'That was nothing more than an indication of my irritation on the day,' Saul told her flatly,

Giselle defended her suspicions. 'You don't want me here.'

'No,' Saul agreed, 'I don't.'

And then he did what he had sworn he would not do, cursing himself beneath his breath as he reached for her, pulling her fiercely into his arms and kissing her with all the pent-up fury she had aroused in him from the moment he had first seen her.

Giselle tried to resist him. She certainly *wanted* to

resist him. But the hand she raised to push him away had developed a will of its own and was sliding along his bare arm beneath the sleeve of his shirt, and the body that should have been arching away from him was instead melting into him.

She was all fire, nectar and ambrosia, heated by her desire to run intoxicatingly through his senses, until he was filled by his need for the scent, the feel, the taste and the sound of her as he coupled her desire to his own. His hand reached for her breast, pushing away the fabric that came between her flesh and his touch with all the urgency and impatience of a young untried youth. The dying sunlight embraced her pale flesh, firing it with its caress, and the ruby darkness of her nipple was a hard thrust of flesh that mirrored in its own way his own taut arousal.

Beneath the pressure of his kiss he could feel and taste her gasp of undeniable response to him. He wanted to devour her, consume her, take her and drive them both until they were equally satiated—even whilst the anger within him that she should make him feel that way roared and burned its resentment of his need.

She was helpless, Giselle recognised, totally unable to withstand the storm lashing at her, able only to cling to the man who was the cause of it and pray that she would survive whilst her body opened all its gateways and let down its barriers to admit the rolling, roiling ferocity that was now possessing her.

This was what she had feared, what she had denied herself for so long, and she had been right to do so, because to suffer what she was suffering now would surely destroy her.

Somewhere else in the building a door banged. The sound exploded into the sensual tension that had enclosed them, driving them apart. Saul's chest was rising and falling as he fought for control; Giselle's whole body was trembling.

Without a word she turned and ran, fleeing as though she was being pursued by the devil himself, not stopping until she had reached her own office, where she quickly gathered up her jacket and her bag, not daring to look behind her as she fled the building.

Saul watched her in silence. He wanted her to go. He wanted what had happened not to have happened. He wanted—

Saul closed his eyes as his body told him exactly what it wanted—no matter what he might think about its desire and no matter how much he might want to reject it. Rolling up the papers Giselle had left behind, Saul slammed them down on the desk as anger against his unwanted physical ache for her savaged his self-control.

CHAPTER FOUR

GISELLE could see from the illuminated face of her small bedside clock that it was almost half past two in the morning, but sleep was impossible. How could she possibly sleep after what had happened? She had no idea why Saul had kissed her. She could only presume it had been his way of punishing her. He had been so angry when she had dared to suggest that he might have tried to trick her.

What had he expected her to do? He had made it plain that he didn't want her seconded to him. He had even said that he would be waiting for her to prove herself not up to the job so that he could demand a replacement for her. Under such circumstances surely anyone would need to be suspicious in order to protect themselves.

In fact for all she knew her suspicions were correct, and his anger could have been because she had not fallen into the trap he had set for her. Had he kissed her as a way of trying to force her to leave? If only she could do just that. If only she could ask, even beg her employers to send someone else to Saul in her place.

She'd picked up a newspaper on her way home, in the desperate hope that by some miracle she might find a job advertised in it that would offer her a means of escape.

She had even gone online to check out some job search websites, but the reality was that nobody was hiring in the current climate—and, much as she hated to admit it, the increased salary Saul Parenti was paying her meant that it would be impossible for her to find another job in London that would pay her as much.

As much as she loathed the blow her pride would suffer every day she had to step across the threshold of the Parenti Organisation, and despite her suspicions that Saul was doing everything he could to manipulate her into leaving, the debt she owed her great-aunt was such that she would just have to bear it. Without her great-aunt… Giselle dreaded to think what would have happened to her if her elderly relative had not stepped in and offered her a home, a safe haven. She had been so kind to her—shielding her, protecting her—but Giselle had caught the small fragments of adult conversations that had dropped to whispers, and then shaken heads and knowing looks when those adults had realised that she was there. She had known they were talking about her, known too of their suspicions about her. As a child she'd had nightmares, dreaming of ghostly voices reaching out to accuse her, and ghostly hands reaching out to drag her down into the darkness.

It had never been discussed between them, but Giselle knew that her great-aunt knew about the secret that could never be spoken. How could she not know when it had been the direct cause of her mother and baby brother's deaths and the indirect cause of her father's? She didn't know the exact details, though—that Giselle had deliberately disobeyed her mother, that she had let go of the pram, pulling back onto the pavement and then watching as the pram's momentum had carried it and her baby brother, and then her mother, who had clutched desperately at the pram's handle, straight under the front wheels of a lorry.

She would never sleep now. She was too afraid of the memories that would surface if she did. She must not go down that dark and tormenting road. She already knew where it led, and the horrors that waited for her at its end.

If only her life could be different. If only right here, right now, there were comforting, loving male arms waiting to enfold her—a strong male chest for her to lean on, and the protection of a man who understood and forgave all that there was to understand and forgive and still went on loving her.

If only there was a man in her life—a lover—whose desire for her and hers for him could prevent her from suffering the sharp pangs of aching sexual need she had felt earlier in Saul's arms, when her body had been on fire with the intensity of what he had aroused within her.

But there wasn't. There never would be; there never could be. The kind of man she wanted to love, the kind of lover she wanted to share such intimacy with, would be the kind of man who carried in his genes a need for the traditional things in life: a relationship, commitment, children.

Children! A shudder galvanised her body. She could not, *must* not ever have a child. And equally she could not and must not ever put a man she might love in a position where loving her back would mean that he would be deprived of his own right to be a parent.

The wilder shores of sexual promiscuity and the supposed 'fun' they afforded were not for her. Even if her
own nature had not inclined her against them, Giselle
suspected that her upbringing by her great-aunt would
have done so.

Until now—until Saul Parenti—she had been free to
believe that her sexuality was under her own control,
and that there was no danger whatsoever of her physical
desire for a man making her want to break the rules she
had set for herself.

Until now.

Those few minutes in Saul's arms, with her senses
hungering beneath Saul's kiss, her flesh clamouring for
Saul's touch, had changed everything. Like a genie let
out of a bottle by a person who did not believe such
things could exist, she was now having to deal with
something that she had believed could never happen.

How was it possible for her of all people to feel such
an uncontrollable flood tide of physical desire for a man
she actively disliked? It went against everything she
knew and understood about herself. Or rather everything
she had *thought* she knew and understood about the
person she wanted to be. Inside her head she could see
once again the small family group: the mother, preoc-
cupied, tense and impatient, the baby—the good child—
sleeping in the pram, whilst she—the bad child—disobeyed her mother's instructions, ignoring them to give
in to her inner need to follow her own instincts. As a
result of that two members of that trio had died whilst
she, the third, had survived.

Since then she had worked unceasingly to be 'good'
and to make amends, but now, thanks to Saul, she was

being forced to accept that the wilful, reckless side of her nature had not been banished at all.

Nothing could be returned to what it had been before Saul's fierce kiss had ripped from her the protection of her own delusion to show her the raw, physical reality of her desire for him.

How had it happened, when she had always been so careful and so controlled? She didn't know. What she did know, though, was that trying to deny its existence would be pointless—as pointless as trying to hold back the tide. It had seared its reality into her senses and sealed itself there with the pain of its white-hot heat. Perhaps this was her punishment for the past? The agonising price she must pay for what she had done? To be tormented by a need that would never be satisfied.

She might not know why she was being forced to endure the agony of physical desire for a man she disliked, and whom she knew disliked her, but what she *did* know was that Saul must never discover her weakness. He must never know that she wanted him, that the desire he aroused in her was overwhelming—and, most humiliating of all, that it was unique in her own experience and felt for him alone.

Like love.

The treacherous thought slid into her mind, to be instantly and frantically denied.

No! What she felt for Saul was nothing like love at all. It was merely physical—physical and nothing else.

Her only comfort was that Saul did not desire *her* with an equally irrational and overwhelming hunger. Because if he did… But, no—she must not go there.

Her eyes were dry and gritty from lack of sleep and

suppressed emotion, and Giselle warned herself that she must try and get some sleep. It was now gone four o'clock in the morning, and she would have to be at her desk for nine—or risk the consequences to her pride. Taking time off because she couldn't bear to face Saul was not an option she was willing to allow herself.

Broodingly Saul stood staring out of his window and watched Giselle as she entered the building. He should not have kissed her. He wished fiercely that he had not done so. Kissing her had breached his own moral barriers against that kind of intimacy with someone he employed—and, even more disturbingly, deep down inside himself he knew that it had also breached his emotional defences. So why make the hole she had driven through those defences even bigger by spending time he should be giving to other things—far more important things—not only thinking about what had happened but actively dwelling on it?

Because he needed to dwell on it—to focus on it and come up with a plan to deal with it and its potential consequences.

Abruptly Saul turned and strode purposefully across his office.

Apprehensively Giselle headed directly for her office, desperate to avoid seeing Saul, only allowing herself to feel safe when she had closed the door behind her with a sigh of relief—only to realise that she was not safe and that Saul was there, standing in the shadows, watching her.

'We need to talk,' he told her peremptorily, not

looking directly at her at all as he crossed over to the window and stood there, looking out of it. His dark-suited figure was highlighted by the light coming in through the window. His back was to her, so that she could not read his expression, but she knew that if he chose to do so he could turn round and see hers exposed by the merciless beam of sunlight pouring into the office.

'What happened between us was a mistake and should not have happened,' he said.

Giselle could feel her pain fanning her anger.

'Do you think that I *wanted* it to happen?' she challenged him. 'Well, I didn't. Because you are who you are, I dare say you believe that all women want to… to be physically intimate with you, and that they hope intimacy will lead to a relationship. Well, I don't. I don't want that and I never will.'

Her angry claim was heartfelt enough to surprise Saul into turning round to look at her.

'It's easy enough to say that, but show me a woman who doesn't claim she wants to be free and then claims that all she's ever wanted is motherhood the minute she's managed to get pregnant by a man she sees as her meal ticket and I'll show you a liar,' Saul retaliated brutally.

His words hit Giselle as brutally as though they had been physical blows, bringing to life her deepest fear.

'I shall never be that woman,' she told him passionately. 'I shall never have a child. *Never!* And as for… for what happened, I wish with all my heart that it had not.'

She meant it, Saul recognized, and he nodded his

head and informed her crisply, 'That makes two of us. For once it seems we are in accord.'

As he strode past her to the door Giselle turned her back to him and pretended to be engrossed in the plans laid out on the large desk beside her.

Back in his own office, though, Saul discovered that neither Giselle nor their kiss was easy to put out of his mind. Last night in his impressively elegant Chelsea townhouse Saul hadn't been able to sleep, despite the comfort of his bed with its stratospherically expensive Egyptian cotton sheets, changed and smoothed to perfection every day by the small and discreet army of service staff provided by the agency he used, because Giselle had got under his skin as effectively as a handful of grit placed under those sheets to deliberately irritate him. And now he couldn't erase her from his thoughts.

In fact her presence in his thoughts had gone way beyond mere irritation, Saul acknowledged, remembering how he had watched the dawn breaking, its grey light coming in through the bedroom window that he preferred to keep open to the light, etching smudged lines across the glass. That dull dawn light would have suited Giselle Freeman, he thought unkindly, with her too-often-washed black suit and her pale hair and skin.

Too late Saul realised his mistake, as the image that immediately formed inside his head was not one that focused on the shabbiness of Giselle's clothes but instead on the way her shirt pulled against her breasts.

His head might be willing to create an unflattering

image of her, but his memory was not being anything as like as co-operative—and as for his body!

Against his will he remembered what it had felt like to hold her. If he closed his eyes now he would almost be able to feel her body trembling against his own, inciting within him the desire to cover her mouth with his and take the sweet, soft movement of her lips hostage. He could imagine the weight of her slender body leaning against his, producing an effect on him as erotic as if she had physically and deliberately placed her hand on his sex and openly caressed him. He could visualise her breasts, naked and revealed for his pleasure. As a young man one of his first sexual experiences had been with an older woman who had liked him to fill his mouth with ice before emptying it to take her hot, swollen nipple into the icy chill of his mouth. She loved the sensuality of his ice-cold mouth against her sex-hot breast. He thought of Giselle, shuddering wildly under such an embrace, her fingers entwined with his as he pinioned her hands back and suckled on her nipples until she was writhing with the pleasure of his caress.

Abruptly Saul dragged his thoughts back under the control of his mind. He'd never been a fan of cold showers, but right now that was exactly what he needed—and being forced to acknowledge that didn't please him one little bit.

Saul wasn't used to anything whatsoever in his life not being under his control, never mind his own body.

It was as though for some reason his own flesh was rebelling against him. What other logical explanation could there be for its maddening insistence on telling him that it found Giselle desirable when he had strictly forbidden it to do any such thing?

Swiftly Saul mentally reviewed the women he had taken to bed over the last five years. He'd never felt any need to prove himself as a man via a list of sexual conquests, but his sexual appetite had been sharpened on and satisfied by some very beautiful women—women who were skilled and adept at appealing to a man's ego, women who did not steal car park spaces nor fill him with an irrational sense of guilt mixed with compassion which was then laced with anger because they wore shabby clothes that made them stand out from their peers in all the wrong ways.

That was it, Saul decided grimly. Put Giselle Freeman in the kind of clothes the other women in his employ wore and, instead of standing out from them, thus forcing him to focus on her, she would fade into the wallpaper, so to speak. Problem solved!

Impatiently Saul buzzed through to his PA and gave her his instructions. He heard her indrawn breath and demanded, 'What's wrong?'

'Saul, if I may say so, I don't think that being told to present herself at Harvey Nichols' personal shopping suite in order to be provided with some new work clothes so that her appearance fits with that of your other female employees will go down very well with Giselle.'

'If she argues, tell her that she doesn't have any choice,' Saul commanded, before ending the call.

He was pleased—not just because he had solved his problem, but because, even more importantly, he felt that he had found the cause for it. He was focusing on Giselle because she stood out from the other women.

Once she ceased to do that he would cease to notice her and when he ceased to notice he would cease to… To want her? He did *not* want her, Saul assured himself. Not really.

Wanting a woman—any woman—was the first dangerous step down a road he had no intentions of travelling. His father had almost worshipped his mother, and look where that had got him. Dead because his mother had refused to give up her aid work and his father had not been able to bear being apart from her. He never wanted to risk loving a woman to that extent. Better by far not to love at all—and that was exactly what he intended to do. He never intended to love and he never intended to have a child. Children were vulnerable—helpless hostages to fate, their emotions so tender that a parent could with the smallest sentence, the briefest gesture, accidentally scar them. He did not want the burden of carrying that responsibility.

His mother, in particular, had been burdened by the responsibility of having him. He could vividly remember how, after a wonderful fortnight spent with his parents, the first summer after he had gone to boarding school, he had begged his mother to allow him to stay with them all the time.

'I could learn from books,' he had told her. 'You could teach me like you teach other kids—you and Papa.'

'No, Saul,' his mother had refused, quietly but firmly. 'If your papa and I were to devote our time to you, then how could we do the work that is so important for helping all the thousands of children who do not have the advantages you have? They have so little and need so much.'

They have you. Saul remembered his eight-year-old self wanting to protest. But of course he had not done so, knowing how much such a comment would have displeased his mother, to whom it had been so important that he understood the needs of the children she worked with from war torn and disaster-struck parts of the world. Children so much more deserving of her time and her love than he himself.

CHAPTER FIVE

'SAUL has done *what?*'

Moira sighed silently to herself as she heard the note of outrage in Giselle's voice.

'He's instructed me to arrange an appointment for you at Harvey Nichols for four this afternoon with one of their personal shoppers. He feels…' The PA paused, trying to find the right words. 'Saul has explained that because of the expense of your great-aunt's healthcare you can't afford to…'

'To what?' Giselle stopped her angrily. 'To buy my own clothes?'

'He simply felt it would be easier for you to fit in if you were provided with some suitable business outfits to wear whilst you are working here. He thought it would help you if—'

'*Help* me? By embarrassing me like this?'

'I don't think for one minute that that was his intention, Giselle.' Moira tried to comfort and placate her. 'In fact I gained the impression that he rather admires you for what you are doing—as indeed I do myself. It can't be easy for you.'

Giselle's body stiffened as she heard the pity in the older woman's voice.

'What can't be easy for me? Wearing cheap clothes? I can think of plenty of things that would be far harder to bear.'

Moira tried another tack.

'A large part of Saul's business comes from the international high finance set, and it is all about convincing them that becoming partners with him and investing in his construction projects will bring them good returns. For that reason he believes that it is important to maintain the right kind of image. We have a mainly young staff, and their standards of grooming tend to be high.'

'So it isn't for *my* benefit that he has given instructions that I am to be shamed and patronised, then,' Giselle challenged her, 'but for his own?'

'For his own *and* for yours,' Moira insisted.

'I won't do it,' Giselle told her fiercely. 'He can get someone else from the firm—in fact I wish he would.'

'Do you? That would mean being sent back to your employers in disgrace. Saul is their most important client. I can understand how you feel, but you have your CV and your future to think of. And with your great-aunt's care to provide, taking any kind of risk with your earning potential might not be a good idea.'

What Moira was saying made good sense, Giselle knew. But that did not mean that she had to welcome hearing it.

The initial surge of adrenalin-boosted fury Moira's announcement had brought subsided now, leaving Giselle feeling emotionally raw and shaky.

Moira put her hand on Giselle's arm. They were in

Giselle's office, where she had come to pass on Saul's instructions.

'I do understand how you must feel, and indeed how I would feel myself, were I you,' she told her calmly.

No, she didn't, Giselle thought inwardly. How could she? How could anyone? *She* was the one who had been subjected to the humiliation Saul was heaping on her. *She* was the one who had been mocked and taunted and…and kissed by him until she was reduced to a molten aching longing.

'I cannot and will not allow Saul to buy my clothes. And since I cannot afford to buy the kind of clothes for myself he seems to deem necessary for those who work for him—'

'It is not Saul who will be paying for them; it is the company. If as an employee you were required to wear a uniform you would not object to your employer providing that uniform for you, would you?' Moira challenged briskly, and continued without giving her time to respond. 'This is just the same. Saul requires you to wear the same "uniform" as his other employees.'

'I won't do it,' Giselle repeated. 'And I shall go and tell him so.'

'You can't,' Moira told her, stepping in front of her as Giselle made to head for the door. 'He isn't here. He's flying to New York this morning. Don't make your mind up right now, Giselle. The appointment isn't until four o'clock.'

This was her punishment for last night, Giselle decided after Moira had gone. She was sure of it.

Her mobile rang whilst she was still brooding on her situation. Her caller was Emma.

'You'll never guess what,' Emma told her without preamble as soon as Giselle had answered the call. 'Bill Jeffries has been called in from annual leave and suspended from work until further notice because Saul Parenti has queried some of his costings. And I should warn you, Giselle, that Bill is blaming you—and gunning for you as well. You're lucky you're working at Parenti's and not over here, I can tell you.'

Listening to Emma, Giselle gripped her mobile more tightly, torn between disbelief that Saul had actually taken her disclosures seriously enough to report them to the partnership for further investigations, the realisation that she must after all have been wrong about him trying to trick her, and the recognition that the door to her escape route from Parenti had just swung closed on her.

An hour later, on her way to the communal coffee machine, one of the other girls smiled at her and asked her if she was settling in okay. Giselle couldn't help but notice how smart Aimee looked. *Her* black suit wasn't shiny from being over-washed—but then it had probably never been anywhere near a washing machine Giselle reflected ruefully. It looked far too expensive for that.

'Saul's gorgeous, isn't he?' Aimee chatted whilst she got her coffee and Giselle queued next to her. 'Pity he's so anti-commitment and settling down. Mind you, if he wasn't I dare say we'd all be trying our best to become the future Mrs Saul Parenti. There's no chance of that, though. Not with him having said so often and so publicly that he intends to remain single and family-free. Oh, it's my birthday at the end of the month—

you're welcome to join us for drinks after work if you're free.'

The other girls here did seem to be welcoming and friendly, Giselle acknowledged, and the drinks invitation was one she would have liked to take up if...

If what? If she could afford to dress like they did?

Some of the coffee she had just made herself slopped over onto the counter as her hand shook betrayingly. It wasn't just expensive clothes that separated her from her co-workers, Giselle reminded herself. There was their differing attitudes to Saul as well. The reason he didn't want to commit and settle down was probably because he couldn't imagine any woman ever being good enough for him, Giselle thought cynically as she made her way back to her office, with her coffee. They seemed eager and ready to adore him, whilst she loathed him.

By three o'clock she had made up her mind what she had to do over the issue of Saul providing her with new work clothes—or rather she had had that decision made for her as a result of Emma's telephone call.

As angry and resentful as it made her, she would have to accept Saul's diktat.

When she went to inform Moira of her decision she couldn't bring herself to meet the older woman's gaze.

Right now there was nothing she longed for more than the financial independence to refuse both this sec-ondment *and* the clothes he deemed good enough to go with it. But of course she couldn't. Not whilst her great-aunt was so financially dependent on her. She owed her elderly relative so much, and nothing—not even her own pride—could be allowed to stand in the way of doing everything she could to repay the debt of loyalty and love she owed her.

Without her great-aunt she would have ended up in a children's home—or worse. Giselle felt the old familiar sickness and fear rising up inside her. It was Saul's fault that she was feeling like this, with her old fears being dragged up from their burial ground to torment her.

Giselle could feel Moira's pity for her in the silence surrounding them.

'It will make your working life here much easier if you can accept that Saul is a law unto himself,' she told Giselle, breaking that silence. 'And that he does not like having his decisions questioned.'

Half an hour later, stepping out into the street, Giselle witnessed a young couple stopping to exchange a tender kiss and her heart turned over inside her chest.

A dangerous emotion was filling her—a sharp, searing feeling of pain and regret because *she* would never be kissed like that, because for her there would never be a time when she was held in a man's arms in an intimate moment of trust and love between them.

That emotion was still worrying her over an hour later, as she sat in the private fitting room of Harvey Nichols' personal shopping suite with a cup of coffee in her hand whilst she waited for the shopper and her assistants to return with a selection of clothes for her to try on.

Why, after so many years of managing perfectly well not to think about all that she would be missing because of her vow to remain single, had her emotions and her body betrayed her now, by reacting in the way that they had done to Saul, of all men?

Her hand shook, spilling coffee onto the skirt of her cheap suit.

What was happening to her? She had always known that there was no escape for her from the burden she must carry. She had known that and accepted it, thankful for the fact that no one else other than her great-aunt knew of the terrible secret she had to conceal. Surely she had been tormented enough by her own guilt? She didn't need the added cruelty of what she had felt yesterday, held against Saul's body.

There was no place in her life and never would be for the age-old instinctive female need for the support of a man strong enough to carry her troubles should she herself grow too weary to carry them. No place either for the white-hot spear of female desire so strong that the ache of it was still pulsing within her.

The problem was that she had grown so accustomed to shutting herself off from what most women would consider 'normal' reactions to the male sex that she had grown complacent, she tried to reassure herself as she drank her coffee. Saul Parenti did not have any special magical powers that made her more vulnerable to him than she was to other men. She had simply allowed her protective guard to slip a little, that was all. Nothing more than that.

The squeak of the wheels of a garment rail being moved alerted her to the fact that the personal shopper was returning. Quickly finishing her coffee, Giselle smoothed down the dark material of her skirt and tried to mask her embarrassment at even being there.

* * *

'We often notice with customers who have lost weight that they find it hard to judge what will be the right fit for them,' the personal shopper informed Giselle with an encouraging smile half an hour later, after she had coaxed her into a black suit, apparently from a designer popular with many working women.

Giselle didn't answer her. She was too busy staring at her own reflection in the full-length mirror. Surely she wasn't really that shape? With that narrow waist and that curve to her hips and her bottom so subtly outlined by the shape of the elegant black skirt? It must be the mirror that was making her look like that. Hadn't she read somewhere that women's fitting rooms had mirrors in them which made customers look slimmer than they actually were?

'Try the jacket,' the shopper encouraged her. 'The skirt's a size eight, but the jacket's a ten because you do have a good bust.'

A good bust? What did that mean?

Giselle soon discovered when she slipped the jacket on and discovered how its shaped shoulders and nipped-in waist accentuated the fullness of her breasts. Panicking, she pulled it off, shaking her head as she told the shopper, 'No, I couldn't wear that.'

'But you looked lovely in it. It was a perfect fit.'

'No. It's too… It was too revealing. I need sensible work clothes that look smart—not clothes that draw attention to my…to my body.'

The shopper laughed.

'I could understand you saying that if I'd brought you some of the more figure-hugging outfits for instance. I have to say that I was tempted, because you have the perfect figure for them. Trust me,' she informed Giselle, 'these pieces will be perfect for you.'

Before Giselle could object again she was producing a crisp fitted white shirt, which she explained had Lycra added to it for a neat fit.

'We recommend a couple of shirts and a couple of plain white short-sleeved round-necked white tees as a basic working wardrobe staple. We're in April now, so I think we should add a lighter-weight skirt—something you can wear with the jacket. Personally I love this black, grey and white patterned skirt.'

Giselle watched with growing discomfort and anxiety as the pile of clothes increased—beautiful elegant clothes—clothes for someone whose life included all the things that hers did not and could not. But there was nothing she could do or say. Saul had given instructions that she was to have a wardrobe suitable for one of his employees, and Moira had warned her not to defy him.

Because if she did he would punish her? How? By kissing her again? By touching her body, her breast, tormenting her nipple until she ached for him to…?

Frantically, her face on fire, her heart thudding, and deep within her that shockingly sensual pulse beating out its message, Giselle struggled to push away her dangerous thoughts.

Three cups of coffee later it was all over, and she and her new clothes—which to her dismay included sheer tights, smart shoes and, most discomforting of all, the underwear that she'd been measured for, having been told by the smiling assistant who did so that despite her narrow back she was a perfect C cup—were being handed into a taxi to be taken home. Even the taxi fare was apparently to be put on the bill, which would be paid by her new employer.

Giselle could feel her face burning afresh at the thought of the accounts department scrutinising the bill for her new underwear. Not so much the thankfully sensible and smooth tee shirt bra, but the other things—the delicate lace and silk bras with matching boy-pant knickers. She had thought at least one of them far too low cut, but the shopper had insisted she was going to need it. How could someone living her life possibly need something so...so sensual and seductive? And as for the two evening dresses that had been included, despite her protestations that she was unlikely to ever wear them...

Her flat was technically in Notting Hill—just. She'd bought it with the money that had been put in trust for her after the death of her parents, which she'd received on her twenty-fifth birthday—just before the recession had really started to bite. On the ground floor of a Victorian house, it included ownership of a tiny back garden, and comprised a good-sized sitting room, two bedrooms—each with its own bathroom—and a kitchen-dining-room which opened out onto the garden.

The previous owners had thoroughly modernised the whole flat, and Giselle hadn't had to do anything other than buy some furniture and move in.

She knew that other women might consider her flat to be bare and lacking in femininity, but she didn't care. A decor that focused on or reflected any kind of female sensual warmth was not for her. It might potentially arouse yearnings and needs she could not allow herself to have. She preferred her home as it was—even if others might think it looked bleak and impersonal.

No photographs or ornaments broke up the flat matt surfaces of the dark furniture. The wooden floors were free of rugs, the leather sofa unadorned by throws or cushions. The bedrooms reflected the same Spartan decor. The entire flat was as immaculate as though no one actually lived in it—but then she didn't really *live* anywhere, did she? Giselle challenged herself as she let herself into the narrow hall, its small space opened up by the large mirrors on the walls, and took all the glossy carrier bags into her bedroom. She didn't really 'live' at all, as other people understood the word.

When she wasn't working or driving north to visit her great-aunt she spent as much time as she could visiting London's museums, walking in the city's parks or just simply sitting in a café watching the world go by. A world of couples and families and happiness from which she was excluded and always would be.

The master bedroom of the flat had the luxury of a walk-in wardrobe. For the first time since its previous occupants had left it would now have something hanging in it that suited its expensive designer space, Giselle reflected as she started to unpack her new clothes. Clothes she knew she would have to force herself to wear.

They were only clothes, she tried to tell herself. She had not chosen them and they were not a gift—rather, they were her own form of personal hair shirt, and that was what she must focus on when she wore them. Not how elegant and smart they made her look, but how painful it was for her to wear them. She must think of them as a penance she was forced to make. A penance forced on her by Saul to punish her.

Giselle's chin lifted. Well, she would make sure that he never knew from her that he had succeeded in humiliating her—again. She would not allow him to know so much as by a look how she really felt. Instead she would make herself act as though she was 'grateful' for his 'kindness', and thus deprive him of any satisfaction he might get from knowing he had got under her skin.

CHAPTER SIX

FROM the glass-sided gallery that ran the full width of his office, Saul could look down into the atrium of the reception area and its busy comings and goings. It was one person his gaze was focused on as she crossed the foyer—Giselle, looking far more smartly dressed than she had done the last time he had seen her.

So she had obeyed his instructions. Good. That of course was the only reason he was watching her—to make sure that she had. So why did the sight of two men from his senior management team turning to watch her walk past with discreet but quite definite male appreciation have his hackles rising like those of a possessive guard dog? Because he did not want flirtations between his staff members distracting them from their work, Saul told himself grimly. That was why.

It was just over twelve hours since he had returned from New York—earlier than he had planned. It was just as well that his business meetings in New York had gone well, Saul reflected, because the situation in another area of his life was going far from well.

He'd received a bewildered telephone call from his cousin whilst he was in New York, from which he had deduced that his cousin Aldo had become the victim of a Ponzi scheme and had probably lost the entire twenty million that Saul had given him when he had realised how hard-pressed financially his cousin was.

Being Grand Duke of one's own country might seem an exalted position, but neither the ducal exchequer nor the country itself was wealthy, and for all his promises of helping out his new son-in-law the Russian oligarch whose daughter Aldo had fallen so deeply in love with and married had so far failed to deliver. Not that Saul *wanted* to see his cousin financially tied to the Russian. It was bad enough that he was already emotionally tied to his daughter.

Saul grimaced with distaste and dislike. There was some history and hostility between Natasha, his cousin's wife, and himself—mainly because he had refused Natasha's advances.

Women! Natasha was a jealous shrew, with no compunction whatsoever about using his cousin for her own ends, and Saul avoided her company as much as he could. Normally he would have tried to sort out the mess in Aldo's affairs without having to visit Arezzio, but on this occasion that would be impossible—which meant that he would have to fly out there. It was a pity he wasn't currently involved with anyone. Another woman clinging determinedly to his side and sharing his bed would help to keep Natasha at bay.

Almost as though it possessed the instincts of a homing pigeon, his attention returned to Giselle and stayed there.

Without him encouraging it to do so his gaze slid over the curve of her hips before travelling upwards, over the white shirt that modestly hinted at rather than revealed the curve of her breasts. What had begun as a mental exercise had turned into something far more personal and intimate with such speed that his body was reacting to his visual scrutiny of her before he could stop it. What the hell was going on? She wasn't his type, her attitude irritated him like that of no other woman he had ever met, rubbing against him like sandpaper, and yet every time he moved to put her in her place something she said or did, something she inadvertently revealed about herself, had him experiencing a pang of sympathy and fellow feeling for her. She was like a thorn under his skin, a pebble in his shoe—an irritant he couldn't escape. Like his growing need to know more about her.

She wasn't just the first but the *only* woman he had ever met who had told him that she wanted to remain single and child-free and meant it. Had she made that decision because, like him, she had been orphaned?

She had stopped still in the middle of the atrium, and was looking round as though she suspected that someone was following her—or watching her? Saul stepped back from the glass. It wasn't like him to allow anyone to get into his head when she had no right to be there. It was because it was well over six months since he had ended his last relationship that he was feeling the increasingly inescapable pulsing ache every time he saw her. Nor could he forget how it had felt to kiss Giselle, to touch her and feel her responding to him as though she too was driven by the same fierce compulsive need that had driven him.

The last woman he had been seeing had started to make assumptions, and with those assumptions demands, which had led to him making it plain to her that he had no intention of making her or any other woman a permanent fixture in his life.

He had thought his parents were permanent fixtures, but they had left him, and their deaths had taught him that nothing and no one could be relied on to always be there. Was that how Giselle felt? Would she understand as no one else had or could that it was impossible for him to risk that level of pain again and survive? If he told her, would she…?

Cursing beneath his breath, Saul reined in his thoughts. He had never discussed his feelings about losing his parents with anyone, and he never intended to do so. It was safer to keep those thoughts to himself. That way it wasn't possible to be hurt, or to feel betrayed when the inevitable happened.

He knew Natasha would undoubtedly hurt and betray Aldo, and probably sooner rather than later. His thoughts returned to his cousin. Yes, Natasha would hurt Aldo— but not through him. Taking another woman with him would definitely help to keep Natasha at bay. His glance returned to Giselle and stayed there whilst he assessed and considered the situation, working with the speed and the focused clarity of a man used to making swift decisions.

'Moira,' he told his PA five minutes later, going into her office, 'I'm going to have to fly out to Arezzio. Fix up a flight with the usual private jet people, will you?'

'When for?'

'ASAP.'

'You've got that lunch appointment with Lord Richards in half an hour,' Moira reminded him.

'Yes. I know,' Saul agreed, and then told her, 'I'll be taking Giselle with me. I've decided I might as well kill two birds with one stone and visit Kovoca as well. I've got some issues with the plans that can best be settled by a site visit.'

After nodding her head, Moira queried, 'Will you be staying on the island? If so, I'll let the caretaker at the villa know.'

'Yes,' Saul confirmed.

It was too late to change his mind now, or to listen to the inner voice that was questioning the reasoning behind what he was doing. Or the reason why she was occupying his thoughts so much. So what if she was? It meant nothing.

Within fifteen minutes Moira was reporting to him that a private executive jet would be waiting on the tarmac at Luton Airport at six o'clock.

Saul looked at his watch.

'I'd better go. I don't want to keep Lord Richards waiting. Tell Giselle she can take the rest of the day off and that I'll pick her up at her home address at three-thirty. That should leave us plenty of time to reach Luton.'

'How long do you expect the trip to last?' Moira asked.

'No more than five days at most—possibly less. I'll be able to be more definite once I've spoken with Aldo and checked properly what's going on.'

Giselle's heart was thudding heavily into her ribs. She was still in shock from learning that she was going to have to accompany Saul on a field trip to Kovoca—a trip she couldn't refuse to go on, since it was quite obviously part and parcel of her work and objecting was out of the question. It would make her look unprofessional and, worse, might lead to Saul guessing that... Guessing what? That she was afraid of being on her own with him because of the way he'd made her feel when he'd kissed her? She couldn't put herself in that position. And she wasn't going to.

Instead she was going to focus on being completely professional. She looked down at her bed and the clothes she had laid out on it. Field trips in her experience usually called for outdoor clothes, which meant jeans, and since she knew from the surveyors' reports that the island's terrain was rugged in places she'd need a pair of sensible shoes.

Moira had warned her, though, that Saul was combining the trip to the island with a visit to his cousin the Grand Duke of Arezzio on what Moira had described vaguely as 'family business'. Giselle looked at her watch. Nearly three o'clock. Moira had said that Saul would pick her up at three-thirty, prior to driving them both to Luton for their flight.

She looked down at the bed again, checking to make sure she'd laid out everything she'd need. Jeans, her two new white tee shirts, undies, sensible shoes—and socks for them—and she would travel in her Joseph work suit and one of her white shirts.

She'd taken the precaution of checking online once she'd got home just to see what the weather would be like in both Kovoca and Arezzio at this time of the year, guessing correctly that it would be warmer than London.

Ten past three. She'd better hurry. The only case she had was the small one she used when she went north for a few days to see her great-aunt.

She had almost finished packing when the doorbell rang. The undies she was holding slipped from her grasp as her heartbeat accelerated. What was she so nervous for? Or was it excitement she was feeling and not nervousness?

Of course it wasn't excitement. Why should it be? The doorbell pealed again, forcing her to hurry to the door.

Saul was standing on her doorstep and a long, dark, polished expensive limousine was parked at the kerb.

'Ready?' he asked her.

'Not quite. Moira said half past three,' she told him defensively, stepping back into her hall and then wishing she hadn't when he followed her inside.

'I won't be long, though, if you want to wait in your car.'

'I never trust a woman when she says she won't be long. Women have a very elastic idea of time, in my experience.'

'That might have more to do with your taste in women than with hard truth about the female sex in general,' Giselle couldn't resist pointing out as she hurried down the corridor, pausing only to turn back towards him and wave her hand in the direction of her living room, inviting him to go in, before assuring him, 'I *will* only be five minutes.'

Saul nodded his head.

He wasn't prepared to admit that he had been curious to see where and how she lived. Picking her up at her home address had merely been effective in terms of the time it would save. Now that he was here, though, he was prepared to admit that it was impossible to learn anything about her life from the impersonal starkness of her decor. Where were the photographs? The cherished bits and pieces of female clutter he was familiar with seeing in the homes of the women he had dated over the years. There was nothing here in this room to tell anyone anything at all about the woman who lived here.

He looked at his watch. Five minutes Giselle had said, and she had one of those minutes left. Opening the door into the hallway, Saul walked towards what he guessed must be her bedroom. The door was open, and he could hear the sound of a suitcase being zipped closed. From the doorway he looked into the room. Like the living room, it was empty of any kind of female frippery, bare and bleak.

'This is your bedroom?' he asked, causing Giselle, who hadn't been aware of his presence behind her until she heard his voice, to spin round immediately to confront him.

'Yes,' she confirmed crisply, almost biting off the word, as though reluctant to make even such a small admission to him.

'It looks more like a nun's cell than a modern woman's bedroom,' was Saul's equally curtly delivered assessment.

The air hissed out of Giselle's lungs as though she

had just taken the full force of a painful blow, but she wasn't about to let him go unanswered.

'That's probably because you're contrasting it with the kind of bedrooms favoured by a *very* different type of woman to me.'

As she spoke both the tone of her voice and her expression made it plain that this 'different' type of woman was, in her opinion, an inferior type.

Reflecting on the women who had shared his bed, and the high value they put on themselves and their needs, Saul had to admit that Giselle had guts—even if she was engaging in a fight for which she was poorly equipped and which, more importantly, he had no intention of allowing her to win.

'Not as different as you might like to think,' he assured her softly, bending down to retrieve from the floor the pair of silk and lace knickers that must have fallen off the bed whilst she had been packing.

Held in Saul's hand, the delicate scrap of nude and cream underwear somehow looked even more deliberately sensual than it had when the personal shopper had insisted on adding it to her purchases.

'A taste for wearing the kind of underwear that a man both likes to see and touch on a woman must be a universal female trait.'

'It wasn't my choice,' Giselle snapped at him as she reached out to take the knickers from him.

But instead of letting go Saul closed his hand round them and enquired, 'A gift from a lover, then, were they?'

'No!' Giselle knew she was losing her self-control to the mix of anger and embarrassment that was storming her, which had been deliberately aroused by this man who was so obviously enjoying baiting her. She wanted to regain that control, but she couldn't. It was like being caught in a fine net—the more she thrashed about, trying to set herself free, the more entangled she became. Like telling lies.

Lies—how they could trick you with their easy offer of security. Like the offer of money from a loan shark. Just like that loan shark, the payment lies demanded for what they had given came with compound interest, to make an intolerable burden that could never be diminished. But how could she ever tell the truth—the whole truth—without being judged and labelled by its darkness herself? She had taken and would continue to take all the steps that needed to be taken to ensure that history could never repeat itself. That was surely all she needed to do?

Saul, watching her, saw the fight drain out of her like blood draining from an open vein. The abrupt change in her from angry adversary to someone who looked too afraid even to breathe didn't bring him any satisfaction, though. His instincts told him that it was not he who had secured a victory, but rather something or someone else.

'You'll need an evening dress,' he warned her, almost absently.

Who or what had caused that almost naked fear he had seen seize her? Why should he want to know or care? He'd always been a man who refused to allow the women he took to bed to bring their emotions into their relationship with him. But he hadn't taken Giselle to bed, and he wasn't having a relationship with her. All the more reason not to question her emotional reactions.

'An evening dress?'

'Yes. Moira must have told you that we will be visiting Arezzio prior to going on to Kovoca?'

'She said that you had some family business to attend to,' Giselle agreed.

'Family business, yes, but you can hardly be expected to eat alone in your room like some Victorian governess. And since my cousin's wife enjoys the formality of being Grand Duchess and dressing for dinner you will need an appropriate outfit. Or were you imagining that I wanted you to dress for me?' Saul taunted her unkindly.

'Certainly not,' Giselle flashed back.

'Good. I wouldn't want you getting the wrong idea just because—'

Gisele stopped him. 'You've already told me that, and I haven't.' She didn't want him mentioning that kiss—not here in her bedroom, where since it had happened there had hardly been a night when she hadn't been woken from her sleep by her memories of it and how he had made her feel.

She was glad of the excuse his assertion that she would need to pack an evening dress gave her to put some distance between them. The cool privacy of her walk-in wardrobe gave her a badly needed opportunity to press her hands to her hot face and try to still her racing heartbeat. Racing because she was so furious, she assured herself, and not for any other reason—not for one minute because her bedroom was now filled with the male smell of the man who had disturbed her dreams for the last two weeks and whose touch was already imprinted on her body and her senses. She reached blindly for the two evening dresses the personal shopper had selected for her, thankful for her sensible advice that the silky jersey fabric wouldn't crush and would be easy to pack.

Whilst he waited for her, Saul studied her bedroom. There was nothing here to give any sense of who or what she was. The room was a blank canvas of anodyne good taste. He wouldn't even have known it was her room apart from one small thing. She might not wear any perfume, but her body carried its own personal scent, recognisable to a man who had held her close, and that scent was elusively and unexpectedly provocatively discernible to him. It reminded him of how she had felt beneath his kiss, of how her body had responded to his touch, her nipples swollen and flushed—

He was doing it again—or rather she was doing it to him again.

Giselle had come back into the bedroom. Saul watched as she unzipped her case and hastily placed the dresses she was holding into it. Her hands were shaking slightly. Watching her, he had a sudden fierce urge to throw the bag onto the floor, then take hold of her hands and place them on his body whilst he stripped hers of its barriers to his possession. What would she do if he did? What would she do if right here and right now he did what his body had been urging him to do virtually from the minute he had set eyes on her?

An overwhelming urge to find out stormed through him, carrying him towards her. He wanted to fill her body with his own. He wanted to take her with him deep into the fire, holding her there until it consumed them both. He wanted... He wanted *her*, Saul recognised.

Giselle refastened her case, and then reached for its handle to lift it off the bed. But Saul beat her to it, picking it up as easily as though it weighed less than her handbag.

Giselle hadn't expected Saul to be driving himself, so was unprepared to be alone with him in the car. It was an unfamiliar experience for her to be sitting in the front passenger seat of a car driven by a man. That was something that couples did—or people who shared some kind of intimacy other than the sort of intimacy they were sharing now, shut away together in the enclosed space of the car's luxurious interior.

Her leather seat seemed almost to shape itself to her body, and the thick-pile carpet was soft beneath her feet. Beneath the expensive leather scent of the car she could smell Saul's skin—not just the cologne he was wearing but his actual flesh, warm, living and male. She could see his hands on the steering wheel, strong and capable hands, with long fingers and clean nails, the skin tanned. Hands whose touch she had felt against her own flesh—but not, of course, in a caress.

What must it be like to sit in a car next to a man, the way she was sitting next to Saul, as his lover? For other women that kind of intimacy—the physical, mental and emotional closeness to a man, a lover—was something they took for granted. But she would never travel through life with a man she loved and who loved her in return. Out of nowhere, a yearning ache of loss welled up inside her. A sense of barren hopelessness that panicked and angered her.

Why should being with Saul Parenti and his...his maleness cause this awareness within her of all that she could not have, all that she could not permit herself to want? He was the very last kind of man she would be attracted to if she was in a position to allow herself to become attracted to someone. Determinedly she dragged her gaze away from him and focused instead on the road ahead, busy now with traffic.

It didn't take them long to reach the airport. As he changed lanes for the airport turnoff, Saul asked, 'Have you already been to Kovoca?'

Giselle shook her head.

'I've seen photographs and video footage of it, and read the surveyors' reports. The land rises pretty steeply on the western side of the island, and with the mountain in the east it makes sense to build the resort on the relatively flat area in between. From the photographs I've seen it looks incredibly beautiful.'

'It is,' Saul confirmed, as the airport buildings loomed up ahead of them. 'Like a green jewel set in a turquoise-blue sea. My grandfather always bemoaned the fact that Arezzio is landlocked, and I suppose that is part of the reason why I bought the island—part, but not all. No man who is controlled by sentiment can ever expect to become successful.'

'And success is very important to you?'

'Very,' Saul agreed, unabashed. 'Any man who denies that he feels the same is lying. Success matters. It feeds the male psyche and it nourishes male pride in much the same way that a man's desire for her nourishes a woman's pride in herself.'

Giselle shot him an infuriated look.

'That is a ridiculously sexist remark, and totally untrue. Women do *not* need to be desired by a man to feel pride in themselves.'

'Maybe not. But when he does, they do,' Saul insisted.

Giselle would have responded and told him what she thought of his ego-bound arrogance if she hadn't suddenly realised that Saul was driving straight towards a gleaming private jet parked only yards away from them on the tarmac.

Giselle had flown in private jets before. The firm had several wealthy clients who thought nothing of flying those they commissioned and employed to wherever they wanted them as speedily as possible. However, there was still *something* about the exclusivity and luxury of stepping out of a car right in front of the plane that was to carry you through the skies that pulled her in two very different ways. There was a distinct thrill and sense of awe about enjoying such privilege, but it came with a feeling of guilt and resentment on behalf of those who could not afford such extravagance.

CHAPTER SEVEN

THE jet was coming in to land. Saul, who had spent most of the flight working, switched off his laptop, the movement drawing the fabric of his shirt tightly across his shoulders and chest. Through the cotton Giselle could see the dark shadowing of his body hair. Her stomach lurched, her muscles tightening in protest against her awareness of his sexuality. She tried to look away from him, but somehow her brain misinterpreted the command she had given it because her gaze slid upwards instead. He'd unbuttoned the top buttons of his shirt and loosened the tie he'd been wearing when they came on board. The five o'clock shadow on his jaw was darker now, its darkness somehow underlining the shape of the male mouth her gaze seemed so eager to focus on, despite her attempts to will it to move away.

Her face burning, Giselle pulled her gaze away. Another few seconds and she'd have been reliving that kiss—again. But even though her instincts screamed for her to think of something else, anything else, she couldn't. And then it was too late for her to do anything other than submit to the sensual memories flooding through her. How was it possible to be so affected by just one kiss? Was it because she had starved herself for so long? Denied herself any expression of her own sensuality? Or was it because Saul Parenti had some special demonic power to affect her that she was power-less to resist?

Saul's voice warning, 'We'll be landing in a minute,' brought her back to reality. Her hands fumbled with her seat belt as she looked rigidly away from him, not daring to look at him in case her body betrayed her and he could see in her eyes what she did not want him to see.

Through the cabin window Giselle could see the countryside over which they were flying. The sun was setting against a backdrop of imposing mountains capped with snow, their lower slopes forested, and the dying light streaked across the calm waters of a large lake.

They were losing height now, and she could see towns and villages clustered in valleys, hugging the edges of the lake, their route following the ribbon of a river tum-bling from the lake into a manmade dam and from there meandering across a broad valley. To her left she could see a sizeable town, with stone bridges spanning the river, a castle built high on a vantage point where an outcrop of rock had resisted the attempts of the river to smooth it away, the mountains rising up behind it. The town had been built at a good strategic point, Giselle recognised.

Beyond the town on the flat delta plain she could see the runway. The plane touched down smoothly as the dying sun began to sink below the horizon in a blaze of pink and gold, leaving the sky richly blue.

A man in a uniform heavily decorated with gold

braid—an official aide-de-camp of some sort, Giselle supposed—lifted a white-gloved hand in an unsmiling salute for Saul as he exited the plane and reached the ground. A red carpet had been laid out, running from the plane to a waiting car.

Although Giselle kept in the background as Saul greeted the uniformed official and shook his hand, she heard the other man saying to Saul, 'Welcome home, sir,' as he escorted them to the waiting car, climbing into the front passenger seat once he had seen them both safely into the opulence of the white leather rear seat.

Since a glass screen separated them from the driver—who was also in uniform—and the official, Giselle felt free to speak to Saul. 'I noticed he said "welcome home" to you. Did you grow up here?'

She didn't *really* yearn to know all there was to know about him. Not one little bit. No, she was simply making conversation so that she wouldn't keep on thinking about that kiss, that was all, Giselle assured herself.

'Not exactly—although Arezzio was home to my father when he was growing up. I did spend some of my school holidays here, though. I was at boarding school in England, and sometimes it was easier for my parents to fly to Arezzio to spend time with me than for me to go and join them. London is where I spend most of my time, although I have my own apartment in Arezzio within the Royal Palace.'

His life was a world away from her own—so much so that they could be living on different planets. And she was *glad* about that, she told herself fiercely. She welcomed everything that reinforced for her how impossible it was for... For what? For her to want him to take her to bed? Her body shook inwardly with the enormity of what was being revealed to her. She must stop thinking like this. She must break free of the spell she was under.

Determinedly she asked Saul, 'Is that the building I could see from the plane?'

'Yes. It was originally constructed as a fortress—some say as far back as the time when the Goths invaded the Roman Empire. But I suspect that that is more legend than truth. Though certainly it dates back to the time of the great castle-building era in Europe. You couldn't see it from the plane, but a new palace was added to the original fortress during the time of the Renaissance—one of my ancestors made a diplomatic marriage with a supporter of the Medicis, and his visit to Florence to woo and claim his bride resulted in him bringing back with him more than a Florentine wife. It is rumoured that she had in her personal retinue a chef who had trained with the chef Catherine de Medici took with her to France, a perfumier, an artist, and several artisans skilled in creating the kind of buildings admired by the Florentines. Apparently she brought her own velvet and silk bed hangings and a good deal more, including her own men at arms and a chest packed with the gold she had coaxed out of her guardian. She was a very ambitious woman, with a desire to create a dynasty.'

'It sounds fascinating,' Giselle told him truthfully.

'My cousin is an academic whose knowledge of such matters is far more extensive than mine. I am sure he will be delighted to show you the records we have of the Florentine bride's dowry.'

As Giselle moved in her seat next to him, Saul felt

his own body responding to her proximity with a fierce male surge of pleasure and desire that caught him off guard. He had never experienced anything like this before, and his instinct for the survival of his emotional independence fought against it just as he was fighting against his body's need.

Giselle felt the movement of air as Saul moved back from her, very obviously putting a distance between them. His action filled her with a sense of desolation that scorched her pride. Had he thought that she wanted to be close to him? Well, she didn't. She moved closer to her own window and stared fixedly out of it, even though there was nothing to see other than darkness now the sun had set.

The lights of the town were up ahead of them.

The town was obviously very old. They drove into it through a bridge tower, and then over a bridge that reminded Giselle of photographs she'd seen of the old Charles Bridge across the river in Prague. Like the Charles Bridge, this one too was decorated with Baroque-style statues and ornamentation.

Once they had crossed the bridge the road opened out into an imposing square, well lit with decorated lamps, whilst the magnificent frontage of the Renaissance building on the opposite side of the square was illuminated by soft floodlighting.

It all looked very imposing and very regal. There was enough light to reveal the flag flying on top of the building—gold-crowned lions rampant against a deep blue background, a Florentine lily between the lions.

The car had come to a halt alongside a flight of stone steps that led to the entrance of the building, its doors guarded by uniformed men, their blue coats the same colour as the background of the flag.

It would be easy to be over-awed by this kind of pageantry, Giselle admitted to herself a few minutes later, when the enormous polished wood double doors were thrown open with a flourish to reveal a large round entrance hall, flooded with light from a chandelier that Giselle suspected was larger than the entire floor space of her flat.

Several sets of doors opened off the hallway, whose walls were painted with the now familiar blue of the ducal arms, and the light from the chandelier crystals splintered and danced on the highly polished wooden parquetry floor. A flight of marble stairs led upwards to a galleried landing, the walls filled with portraits of autocratic, arrogant-looking men who all bore a strong resemblance to Saul. But it was the woman standing halfway up the stairs who drew and kept Giselle's attention.

She was, Giselle thought, quite simply the most beautiful-looking woman she had ever seen. Tall and slender, with thick, dark shiny hair that fell to her shoulders and framed the perfect symmetry of her face. It didn't need the jewels round her throat and wrists or the fit of the gown she was wearing to tell Giselle that this was a woman who was used to the very best of everything.

'Saul.' Her lips formed a smile as she almost purred Saul's name.

Her eyes were the same shade of rich sherry as the silk dress she was wearing. She descended the stairs with graceful ease, standing in front of Saul in such a way that Giselle, who had been standing at his side, was forced to step back onto a lower step, excluded from the intimate circle the other woman was forming with the angle of her body. Her hand was on Saul's arm, her diamond-set wedding band and the huge solitaire she was wearing with it glittering as they caught the light.

There was a predatory possessiveness about her attitude to Saul, Giselle recognized. An intimacy that brushed coldly against her own senses, causing her to feel an inner disquiet and revulsion—because already Giselle was sure that this woman was Saul's cousin's wife. And she was equally sure that she desired *Saul*.

Without seeing his face it was impossible to see whether or not he reciprocated her desire, but surely no man could fail to be tempted by such beauty—and availability?

Giselle took another step down the stairs, and then went rigid with shock when out of nowhere Saul's hand curled round her arm, pulling her back towards him. Automatically Giselle tried to pull away, but Saul wouldn't let her. She could see the way in which Natasha's gaze had fastened on Saul's hand on her arm.

'I thought you'd be coming alone,' Natasha said to Saul. 'Since Aldo has such important and private family business to discuss with you.'

'You thought wrong.' Saul's answer was unequivocal. 'Where is Aldo?' he added.

'He's in the library—where else?' Natasha gave a petulant shrug. 'I am bored with these books he finds so fascinating, and I have told him so. But soon I shall have some fun as my father has a new yacht and I am to spend the summer on it as his hostess. You must join us,

Saul. My father will introduce you to many influential people. There is good business to be had in Russia for those with the right connections.'

'I'm afraid that my plans for the summer depend very much on what Giselle wishes to do, Natasha.'

Saul's voice held anything but regret, but it wasn't that that had Giselle turning to him with a shocked demand for an explanation on her lips. He silenced it by nipping her arm sharply.

'Goodness.' Natasha's smile was as deadly as arsenic. 'Your new friend really must have some very special talents if you envisage still enjoying her in three months' time, Saul. You don't normally keep your lovers that long.'

If she *had* been Saul's lover then his cousin's wife's offensive remarks would have been bound to cause her distress and anger, Giselle knew, but right now it was Saul who was the cause of those emotions, not Natasha. What on earth was he doing? Why hadn't he told the other woman that theirs was a business relationship? Giselle looked accusingly at him, ready to correct Natasha herself, but there was a look in Saul's eyes that warned her against doing so, reminding her of just how much she was already in his power, and how dependent financially she was on his good will, no matter how much she might resent that reality.

'Tell Aldo that I'll talk with him later, will you, Natasha?'

'Later? Why can't you talk to him now?'

'You've just said that he's busy—and besides, it's been a long week. I've been in New York and Giselle has been in London. We've got a lot of catching up to do.'

As he spoke Saul turned to give Giselle a look that said quite openly that the kind of catching up he had in mind involved a bed and Giselle's body naked for his enjoyment in it. Even though she knew that look was manufactured and meant nothing, and even though she was furious with him, it still had the power to melt through her resistance and leave her quivering inwardly on the edge of a quickening pulse of desire that arced and ached almost painfully inside her.

It was plain that Natasha was equally aware of what Saul had wanted to convey. Her lips pressed together and her gaze hardened on them both—but especially on her, Giselle recognised.

'Dinner is at ten o'clock,' she announced coldly.

'We'll try and make it,' Saul responded. 'But don't hold anything up for us. Go ahead without us. Like I said, we've got a lot of catching up to do.'

Natasha's face was a picture—a furiously angry picture, Giselle acknowledged. And she wasn't the only one who was furiously angry with Saul either. He'd put his arm around her now, and was guiding her towards the stairs, probably refusing to let go of her in case she demanded an explanation for his behaviour in front of Natasha, Giselle decided, reluctant to admit that she might well have done so if she hadn't taken such an immediate dislike to the other woman.

CHAPTER NINE

'I want to know what's going on,' Giselle demanded as soon as she felt they were out of earshot of Natasha. As she spoke she tried to pull away from Saul, but once again he refused to let her go.

'Not yet,' he answered as they reached the top of the stairs. 'This way.'

The walls of the wide corridor were hung with more portraits. They paused several doors opening off it before they finally reached a set of imposing double doors that blocked off the whole corridor.

When Saul produced a key to unlock the doors Giselle tried not to look surprised, but she recognised he was aware of her reaction when he turned to her as he unlocked and opened the door and told her succinctly, 'I consider this apartment to be just as much my private space as my London home, and as such I prefer it to remain exactly that—private. Ludmilla, the housekeeper, has been here for almost as long as I can remember, as have many of the staff. She has a key, and I know I can trust her with it.'

Meaning that there were those he could not? Natasha, for instance?

The room beyond the double doors had all the

elegance one would expect in such a building, with its baroque design and decor, but it was in a stripped-back way that was unexpectedly pleasing to both the eye and the senses. The wood-panelled walls were painted a soft grey, plain off-white curtains hung at the windows, and the mirror above the fireplace reflected the room's few pieces of what Giselle suspected must be very valuable antique furniture. The heavy Knole sofas, covered in a matt grey and cream damask velvet, had highly polished tables behind them, with lamps with dark grey shades, and the carpet was obviously old, with beautifully soft shades of creams and blues woven into a design that echoed the ornately plastered ceiling. The light from a chandelier filled the room, throwing softly delicate shadows.

It was a masculine room, but one in which a woman could enjoy and appreciate her surroundings, Giselle recognised, immediately clamping down on her thoughts as she realised where they might be leading.

'Your room is this way,' Saul told her.

Her room? So, despite what he had implied to Natasha, he had no real intention of them being lovers. But of course she had known that. Known it but wished it was otherwise? Of course not.

'I'm not going anywhere until you tell me what's going on,' she repeated, 'and why you let Natasha think...'

'Think what?'

'You know perfectly well what. You implied to her that we are lovers.'

'Yes, I did.'

His unexpected admission had Giselle momentarily

unable to think of any response other than a weak, protesting, 'Why?'

'Isn't it obvious?' Saul challenged with a small shrug. 'You've seen Natasha. You've heard her. She makes it very obvious what she wants, I would have thought.'

What he meant was that Natasha had made it very obvious that she wanted him, Giselle knew. An attack of helpless, hopeless emotion gripped her by the throat and shook her like a rabid dog shaking its prey. Surely she wasn't feeling jealous and desperate because Natasha wanted Saul and was so obviously much more his kind of woman than she could ever be? Was this what wanting Saul had reduced her to? *Wanting* him? How could such a mundane word possibly express the agony of what had been happening to her since he had kissed her? The savage aching pain of the need that had grown so intense that it woke her from her sleep to possess her body and undermine her defences?

Out of her despair, Giselle said the only thing she could think of say to protect herself. 'You must have given her some cause to believe that her…her feelings would be reciprocated,' she accused. Just as he had done to *her* when he had kissed her. With a man like Saul that was all it took to turn a woman into an aching misery of desire—one kiss. As she knew.

'No. Never,' Saul defended himself curtly.

'If that's true, why don't you simply tell her that you aren't interested? Instead of…of taking refuge behind a fake relationship with me.'

'Natasha is married to my cousin,' Saul responded. 'He loves her. He is besotted with her, in fact, and he believes that she loves him in return. The truth is that

Natasha turned her attentions to Aldo and pursued him after I had made it plain that she was wasting her time pursuing me. Natasha does not like being refused what she wants. She's perfectly capable of blatantly breaking her marriage vows, and I wouldn't put it past her to lie in wait for me in my bed if she thought that would get her what she wants.'

'And would it?'

Giselle could see from Saul's expression that she had angered him—again. Would he punish her this time as he had done before? By kissing her? The rush of sick longing that burst through her left her feeling weak and distraught. She hated herself for what was happening to her even more than she resented Saul for causing it to happen.

Panicking, she accused him, 'You planned this all along, didn't you? You brought me here intending to use me, to sacrifice my professional status, by pretending that I'm just another silly fool who wants to crawl into your bed and can't think of anything else. You are every bit as immoral and devious as your cousin's wife. The two of you deserve one another. You probably really do want to sleep with her.'

Was that really what Giselle thought of him? That he was the kind of man who would betray his closest blood relative? It shocked Saul to realise just how much her opinion of him mattered to him. He took a step towards Giselle, and then stopped as she in turn stepped back from him.

'Yes, I did bring you with me partly in the hope that your presence would make it plain to Natasha that I am not interested in her—which I am not.'

'Only partly?' Giselle challenged him. 'So what are the other reasons?'

Hell, but he wanted her—right here, right now, her mouth under his, her body beneath his, his hands free to explore every centimetre of her. Saul's heart slammed into his ribs. He wanted her, and if he didn't get out of here and fast he wouldn't be responsible for what might happen.

So why, instead of taking her to her room and leaving her there, was he stepping up to her and deliberately taunting her. 'Are you hoping secretly that it's because I want to take *you* to bed?'

'No!'

She was saying no, but the look in her eyes, the convulsive movement of her throat, the rise and fall of her chest betrayed her, so that suddenly and searingly Saul knew that against all the odds she shared the unwanted need that was driving him. There could be no other explanation for that wild, frantic, helpless look of mingled rage and longing in her eyes that portrayed so exactly what he was feeling himself.

Saul had guessed how she felt and he was tormenting her, ready to humiliate her—again, Giselle decided, and was panicked into another fierce, 'No!' before adding for extra emphasis, 'You would be the *last* man I would want as my lover.'

That was enough—more than enough, Saul recognized—to breach the dam of his self-control.

'Liar,' he breathed against her lips as he took her in his arms. 'This is what you want, what we *both* want and need,' he told her.

Giselle was lost, helpless to protect herself, helpless

to resist the torrential flood of her own desire-laden reaction to his words and to him.

In his arms her body melted. Beneath his lips her own parted. She clung to him as pliable and responsive, as eager to meet and match his every need as though she had indeed been formed from one of his own ribs and was thus part of him—owned by him, given over to him. Everything that was not Saul ceased to matter. Everything other than her own need for him, which was now possessing her, driving her, consuming her.

Her own need… Just before her world of reality and logic spun off its axis, flinging her headlong into a new galaxy of previously unimagined and undreamed-of sensations and pleasures, her final shocked recognition was of just how much she wanted and needed what was happening. How much she wanted this and Saul himself, and how right he had been to mock her denials.

She tried to pull back, panicked by and afraid of her own vulnerability, recognising at a deep instinctive level her own danger, and yet at the same time filled with an equally intense longing to continue the kiss, to let it and Saul take her to that place her body now yearned to reach.

Beneath the possession of his mouth Saul felt her hesitation and looked down into her eyes, which like his own were open. In their smoky depths he could see confusion clouding the open heat of her arousal. He could see in those bewildered desire-clouded eyes everything that he was feeling himself.

He wanted, he recognized, to hold her, to wrap her in his arms and tell her that he too was confused and afraid, that he too did not understand how things had come to this or why, that he too wanted to reject what he was feeling and could not do so. He wanted to hold her protectively and go on holding her, to comfort and reassure her, but at the same time he wanted to strip from her every last vestige of her self-control until the pure essence of her was his for the taking.

This was not merely physical desire that was driving him, Saul recognised. Emotions that were unfamiliar to him but which he knew must have been buried somewhere deep within him had unfurled themselves inside his heart, and the sensation of them doing so and his own recognition of them was almost physically painful.

He felt Giselle shudder in his hold and instinctively tightened his arms around her. He wanted to tell her that there was nothing to fear, but at the same time he knew that they both had everything to fear from what was happening. He wanted to tell her that she could trust him, that he would not let her fall nor fail her, and that in his arms she would be safe and protected—but how could he when he could not trust himself?

'No!'

Giselle's shakily breathed denial mated with his own harshly countered, 'Yes.'

The sound of their voices entwined as Saul was entwining his fingers with Giselle's, as inside his head images of her body writhing sensually against his entwined with scattered hot darts of erotic punishment against his flesh like pellets from a shotgun, to leave their mark on him and within him, stinging him into swift retaliation as he bent her to his will beneath the heated pressure of his kiss. Her skin felt sweetly soft beneath his fingertips. Her breathing was unsteady, and a tiny frantic pulse was beating beneath her skin. Like a man in a dream he smoothed the pad of his thumb over the soft swell of her bottom lip and felt it quiver in response. A fine tremor, no more, that spoke far more tellingly to his senses than any more overt response could ever have done.

It was too late to draw back now—too late to do anything other than submit to her need and to Saul's mastery of it, Giselle decided helplessly, and a small inarticulate moan bubbled in her throat as his tongue-tip probed her lips.

Was her moan a sign of refusal or a sign of acceptance? He wasn't sure. What he was sure of was that when he kissed her Giselle moved closer to him, accepting him, surrendering herself to him. What had started out in anger had within the space of a few heartbeats become very different—for both of them.

The tormenting movement of Saul's tongue was more than Giselle could bear. The ache Saul had unleashed inside her was too much. Giselle reached for him, her fingers tightening into the muscles of his upper arms and then his shoulders, as she tried to increase the contact of his tongue-tip against her tormented flesh. For a second there was nothing, and then there was everything—his mouth on her own, his hands holding her, moving over her, bringing her closer to him.

The heat of her own desire flooded through her, her toes curling up inside her smart new shoes, her nipples peaking stiffly beneath her silky bra, a sensual pulse beating threadily and intimately within her.

The minute she lifted her hands to the nape of Saul's

neck to hold him even closer to her *his* hands slid beneath her jacket and skimmed her body, fleetingly and delicately, in the merest brush of a caress. But it was still enough to sensitise her nerve-endings and make her skin tingle. Her lips parted beneath his on a soft gasp of pleasure, swiftly captured and just as swiftly interpreted and answered as his hands returned to her body, stroking just as lightly, but this time lingering appreciatively on the curves of her breasts. Stroking and then holding them.

Giselle opened her eyes and looked down, the sight of the tanned flesh of Saul's lean hands cupping her breasts making her shudder wildly with a pleasure that was all the more intense for her having seen as well as felt her body's desire for him.

Never had he felt such a sweetly open, helplessly sensual response to such a small caress, Saul knew. And never, *ever* had his own body reacted with such a powerful surge of male arousal, or felt such an aching urge to take possession. If she could respond to such a light caress so intensely what would her response be when he laid her bare to his touch and his taste? When he held her and drove them both to the ultimate fulfilment?

The temptation to find out rolled through him and over him. His fingers unfastened her blouse, freeing her breast from its silk imprisonment into the possession of his caressing touch whilst his lips teased and tugged at hers until they parted on a soft moan of pleasure and his tongue was able to set a slowly sensual rhythm within the wetness of her mouth that matched the tug of his fingers on her engorged nipple.

Heat, wet and urgent and intense, was spreading

through her, melting her insides, feeding the growing impatient pulse that was beating through her body and commanding that every cell within her followed its lead.

In the lamplit room Saul's gaze feasted on the perfect shape and the pale flesh of Giselle's breasts, their paleness contrasting with the swollen flaunting darkness of her nipples. The ache of his own tautly aroused sex pulsed fiercely, fighting against his self-control, whilst his hands moved lower to push her skirt out the way.

Giselle watched him in a daze, her attention focused on the swift skilled movement of his hands that said how familiar he was with women's clothes and their fastenings. She had no will to move or speak. All her rational response systems had shut down. She felt as though she were standing apart from herself, as though she had become a different person—a person who wanted and ached for the intimate touch Saul's swift despatch of her skirt promised.

Beneath the delicate silk of her underwear Saul could see the soft mound of her sex, rising from the slightly concave flesh that surrounded it so that it could signal the presence of the sensuality it covered. Silk on silk was the sensation relayed to his own flesh as he stroked her briefs against the feathering of her pale body hair, his thumb probing the low-lying hipline of her underwear whilst his fingertips found the bare flesh of her thigh just beneath the leg of the briefs.

The heat and wetness of her own desire would at any other time have shocked and embarrassed her, Giselle thought wildly, but right now the message they were sending out to her was one that clamoured for the sensation of Saul's more intimate touch, making her lean wantonly towards him.

In response Saul took hold of her hand with his own free hand and placed it against his erection. His other hand slid inside her briefs as he did so, to cup her soft eager flesh and then slide fingertips into the wet heat the aroused outer lips of her sex had opened so eagerly to offer him.

As he explored her Giselle's hand tightened on his erection and clung to it, caressing it with urgent, eager movements that reciprocated the rhythm with which he was arousing her. She longed for them both to be rid of their clothes so that she could be free to explore all of him—and not just with her hands. She wanted to breathe in the scent of him, to stroke her tongue-tip over the ridges of male muscle and flesh that made up his body, to arouse him up to and then past the point of madness as he was surely already doing to her.

He couldn't hold out much longer, Saul knew. Right now all he wanted to do was spread the soft willingness of her thighs and sink himself into her, over and over again, until she rose and fell against him with the song of her arousal filling his ears and the climax of her orgasm compelling from him the hot, wet exultation of his own satisfaction.

He bent his head and took her nipple into his mouth, licking and nipping erotically at the taut flesh, pressing his free hand flat against Giselle's upper back so that he could rock her with deliberate sexuality against both his mouth and his fingertips. He suckled deeply on her breast, stroking her clitoris.

Somehow, with a need born more of urgency than

skill, Giselle had managed to unzip Saul's trousers, and now her hand was enclosing the hot rigid tip of his sex. The male flesh moved erotically within her caress, eliciting a groan from Saul that was gasped against her breast. His response to her intimacy caused Giselle herself to shudder wildly at the raw sensuality of what Saul was doing to her. Hungry for him, she pressed closer to him, moving her body against his hand, moving her own hand against his flesh, her arousal increased by the mingled sounds of their shared sensuality, by the probing pleasure-giving fingers moving over eager, hot, wet flesh, the accelerated breathing and raw betraying groans of male desire-driven need.

She cried out when Saul's mouth abandoned her breast, but the sound was quickly stifled by the intimacy of the probing, thrusting kiss he gave her, and the knowledge that soon soon now the rhythmic movement of his tongue against her own would be mirrored by the possessive male thrusting of his body filling her own.

As though she had spoken her longing aloud, Saul's hand reached for the top of her briefs. A wave of heat and excitement engulfed her. She couldn't wait for the pleasure she knew there was going to be—and then it happened. The sharp, intrusive ring of Saul's mobile cutting through their shared intimacy like acid.

For a handful of seconds Saul tried to ignore the shrill demand, but the phone was in his jacket, which he had dropped on one of the chairs when they had first entered his private quarters, not close enough to hand for him to silence it without releasing Giselle.

'You'd better answer it. It might be something important.'

As she spoke Giselle felt as though she was breaking the protective bubble that had enclosed her, and
now—sharply and horribly—she was acutely aware of
her own nakedness and mortification. It was different
for Saul. All he had to do was discreetly zip himself up
as he reached for his phone. Giselle was thankful that
at least he had his back to her as he answered it, thus
giving her the chance to struggle awkwardly back into
her own clothes, whilst she heard him speaking.

'Yes, Aldo. Natasha did say that you were in the library. Yes, of course I can come down and talk to you
now. Just give me five minutes and I'll be with you.'

The cruel lash of reality had stripped the warmth
of sensuality and desire from Giselle as easily and no
doubt as uncaringly as Saul had all but stripped her
clothes from her, she acknowledged miserably, writhing
inwardly. How could she have behaved like that? How
could she have been so lost to everything she believed
in about herself and about the way she had to live her
life?

'I've got to go. But first I'll show you to your room.'
Saul didn't dare allow himself to look at Giselle as he
replaced his mobile in his jacket pocket. If he did then
he didn't know if he would be able to keep his promise
to his cousin—because if he looked at her with his body
aching for her in the way that it was he didn't think he'd
be able to walk away from her.

How had it happened? How had he come to allow a
woman to burn through his self-control and make him
want her so intensely that nothing else mattered? How
had he allowed it to happen? Saul grimaced. He hadn't
had any kind of control in the matter. He hadn't been

capable of allowing or not allowing anything. The truth was that he still wasn't. One word from Giselle—one look, one small sound—that was all it would take for him to reach for her. And that was why he couldn't trust himself to look at her.

Silently Giselle followed Saul until he opened a pair of double doors that led into another room—a library this time. Saul strode through it so quickly that she didn't have time to give it anything more than a cursory look. Saul was opening another set of double doors that led from the library into a rectangular hallway, with one flight of stairs going up from it, and another leading downwards. He hadn't looked at her once as they had traversed the large, elegantly furnished rooms with their stucco-plastered and painted ceilings and their antique furniture, and Giselle told herself that she was glad that he hadn't, ignoring the ache of unsatisfied desire eating into her that gave the lie to her mental claim.

'This apartment has its own entrance,' Saul was informing her, his voice clipped and formal, his manner towards her chillingly distant. 'The doors on the opposite side of this hallway lead to a dining room, and beyond them is a kitchen. Like me, my parents also valued their solitude and their privacy.'

Was that meant to be a warning to her not to read anything into the intimacy they had just shared? If so, there was no need for it. After all, she had her own reasons for knowing there could never be any true intimacy between them. No true intimacy, maybe—but, oh, how her body ached and, yes, screamed inwardly for the release and satisfaction it had been denied. A satisfaction that she would have had if only Saul's mobile had rung a handful of minutes later, Giselle was sure.

That she should have such thoughts was wrong, and surely shamed her, but her body was refusing to be shamed. It wanted her to close the distance between Saul and herself. It wanted— No. No, she must *not* let herself feel that way. Instead she should be relieved—glad that Saul had stopped when he had. Shouldn't she? She was on the pill, after all, prescribed for her a couple of years ago for her erratic periods, and she had continued to take it even though there was no contraceptive need for her to do so. There was no danger of her conceiving. No danger of either of them creating a situation they didn't want, since neither of them wanted any kind of commitment.

Why couldn't she have the appetite Saul had conjured up in her satisfied? Why shouldn't she know his possession?

Saul had started to climb the stairs, and was obviously waiting for her to do the same.

'On the next floor there are four bedrooms, each with its own bathroom. I've made arrangements for a guest-room to be prepared for you,' he was telling her, still in that same clipped and distant voice that told her quite clearly how little he wanted to return to the intimacy they had been sharing.

He was probably relieved and grateful that they had been interrupted, Giselle told herself as she reached the top of the stairs and a galleried landing with corridors running either side of it. Dutifully Giselle followed Saul down one of them to a door at the end which he opened for her.

Taking great care to avoid coming into contact with him, Giselle stepped into it, her private misery briefly eclipsed by the discovery that the bedroom looked like something out of one of the National Trust houses her great-aunt had so loved visiting.

A feminine-looking tester bed was draped with hangings in blue and cream patterned silk that echoed the colour of the patterned carpet and the painted panelled walls. Giltwood furniture decorated the room, and included a chaise longue at the bottom of the bed and a pretty desk and chair. Two rather more solidly comfortable-looking chairs were drawn up on either side of the fireplace, and either side of the bed was a pair of double doors.

'The doors lead to a bathroom and a dressing room,' Saul informed her, adding, 'Dinner won't be until ten, if you recall.'

Giselle nodded her head, and watched as Saul turned and left the room.

In London, even though he was the boss, the gulf between them hadn't seemed anything like as huge as it felt right now, as she recognised how very different their worlds were. Not that it mattered, of course. How could it? Just because of…of what had happened, the sensual intimacies they had shared, it didn't mean anything. Not to Saul. She already knew that. And the fact that she had enjoyed, even welcomed those intimacies did not mean anything either. It couldn't and it mustn't—not now and not ever.

Only now could she relax and allow herself to breathe properly, let her body tremble with the need that still ached through her. Giselle sank down onto the bed. How could this have happened to her? Why had it happened? Why should life be so cruel to her? Hadn't she already suffered enough? Hadn't she already been punished enough? Dark thoughts of hopelessness and despair swirled dangerously inside her head—thoughts of there being no point to anything, not even her own existence. But she must not think like that. That way lay terrible danger.

Panicking, Giselle got up from the bed. She must find something to do that would redirect and occupy her thoughts, restore them to…to… To what? To sanity? The sanity that had been denied her? But, no—she must not go down that route. Where was her laptop? She needed to work, to be professional, to think only about those things that did not involve her emotions.

An exploration of the bathroom and dressing room revealed two rooms both larger than the bedroom in her flat. The bath, she'd discovered, was huge and traditional, with claw-shaped feet, and stood in dignified solitude in the middle of the white tiled and gilt mirrored bathroom.

Someone had already unpacked for her, hanging the few clothes she had brought with her in one of the wardrobes that filled two walls of the dressing room. Her laptop case had been carefully placed on the dressing table stool, and Giselle seized on it with grateful relief, her hands trembling as she unzipped the case and removed her laptop.

Work—work was the panacea and the cure, the antidote for the disease that was threatening her. How could she have let things get so out of control? Things? By *things* did she mean her own desire, her longing, her aching, her need for Saul's touch, for his possession, for his…? Blindly pushing the laptop away from her, Giselle started to pace the dressing room.

He might be listening to Aldo, but his mind wasn't fully focused on what his cousin was saying to him, Saul knew. Instead his thoughts, like the ache that still tormented his body, belonged to Giselle.

How had it happened? How had a woman who had begun by irritating and infuriating him somehow developed the power to infiltrate his thoughts and his senses to such an extent that her presence there overwhelmed everything else? What was she doing? Was she aching as much as he was? Was she thinking about the pleasure they would have shared if they hadn't been interrupted?

'Natasha's father has offered me the opportunity to invest in a diamond mine he has recently added to his investments. If I can manage to get something back from this Ponzi scheme Natasha wants me to go ahead, but Ivan cannot confirm that the diamonds are being mined ethically,' Aldo was saying.

His comments caused Saul to grimace derisively to himself at the thought of Natasha's father being involved in *anything* that was remotely ethical. Not for the first time Saul wished that his cousin had not fallen under Natasha's spell.

'I'll provide you with enough money to cover all your outgoings,' Saul assured Aldo. 'I just wish you had consulted me before getting involved with the scheme.'

'I was going to, but Natasha said that there was no need. Now, of course, the poor darling feels absolutely dreadful and is convinced that you will blame *her*. You mustn't, Saul. If I was more of a man—more like you, more the kind of husband she deserves—then I would have realised the danger for myself. It isn't Natasha's fault that she is married to such a weakling and a failure.'

'You are neither of those things, Aldo. You are a good ruler, a good husband, and when you and Natasha have a child you will be a good father, the best of fathers, because you will be here for your children.'

When Aldo shook his head, Saul's heart ached for him. A woman like Giselle would *never* shame and humiliate the man to whom she had committed herself and her future in the way Natasha was doing to his cousin.

That knowledge, and just as shocking the thinking that lay behind it, froze Saul to his chair. What the hell was he doing, linking such thoughts together? The three words, Giselle, commitment and future, felt as though they were etched in fire inside him, producing an indigestible truth he didn't want to acknowledge. Against all the odds, against everything that he had always promised himself, somehow a link had been made between Giselle and his emotions.

That link must be dissolved and destroyed.

CHAPTER NINE

It was no good her trying to work. She couldn't. Giselle sighed in defeat. What had happened couldn't be pushed out of her thoughts and under a carpet of other busy thoughts and actions, no matter how much she wished it could be.

She looked at her watch. Nine o'clock. What was Saul doing now? Was he with his cousin? With Natasha? Jealousy as swift and sharp as any serpent's fangs bit sharply into her heart. This was wrong, Giselle told herself. What she was feeling was wrong.

A sudden knock on her bedroom door had her stiffening and staring at it. Saul. He had come back. To finish off what they had started? The emotion that flamed through her wasn't denial or reluctance or any of the things it should have been. Instead it was yearning and delight and excitement.

She was halfway out of the chair when the door opened—only it wasn't Saul who had knocked on it, it was Natasha, and her appearance deflated Giselle's emotions as effectively as a pin piercing a child's balloon.

The other woman looked as though she was already dressed for dinner, the red dress she was wearing a perfect foil for her olive skin and dark colouring. It clung so tightly to her body that it left little to the imagination. Were her breasts real? Giselle found herself wondering. Or had they been surgically enhanced, as her Jessica Rabbit-shaped body seemed to suggest? She was wearing a collar of rubies and diamonds round her neck that must have cost a fortune, and matching bangles on both wrists. Her hair was swept up to fall in perfectly coiffured curls, her make-up was immaculate, and her nails were painted exactly the same shade of scarlet as her dress.

'I just thought I'd take the opportunity of having a word with you whilst Saul is talking to Aldo. You know, of course, that Saul will never commit to you and that you won't have a future with him?'

'Yes, I do know that,' Giselle agreed. It gave her a certain amount of unsisterly satisfaction to see that her response had not exactly pleased the other woman.

'And you don't mind? You don't care that he is only using you for sex, and that he will discard you once he grows bored with you? That he will never commit to you and most of all never, ever allow you to have his child? He wanted me for himself, but he felt obliged to step aside once he realised that Aldo wished to marry me.' Natasha continued, without giving Giselle the chance to say anything. 'Saul will never marry, you see. He will never marry and he will never have a child, especially a son, because he knows that his son will have to take second place to mine and Aldo's son…when we have one.'

She paused, a small hint of a frown marring her perfectly smooth face as though something displeased her, before continuing, 'Just as *he* has had to take second place to Aldo. Of course his pride cannot bear that thought. Saul has to come first in everything. As a child, the eldest born of a second son, he grew up resenting having to stand in Aldo's shadow. That is what drives him now. If I were you I would find myself someone else.'

She had turned away and was opening the door before Giselle could say anything to her. Had she herself been someone who hoped for commitment from Saul, someone who desperately craved the joy of bearing the child of the man she loved, then Natasha's cruelly calculated words would have destroyed her hopes and dreams. If she had been that someone. But she wasn't, and instead Natasha's assertion and the ring of truth it had held unleashed within her a potent mix of emotions and an intoxicating sense of being set free from the restrictions she had previously placed on herself.

Although Natasha didn't know it, what she had said to her about Saul made him the perfect man for Giselle. No. Not the perfect man, but the perfect lover. Now she could admit and accept the torrent of longing that was possessing her—now she could open the floodgates and let it surge and soar within her. Now, if Saul should approach her, she could surely allow herself to touch the fire and let it consume her without any fear for the future.

It was past nine. Time she got ready.

Once she had showered, Giselle went into the dressing room and opened the wardrobe, taking out the two evening dresses. Evening dresses provided and paid for by Saul. They weren't anything like as provocative as the dress Natasha had been wearing, but they were stylish.

They were dresses for a woman confident about herself, about her sensuality, and about the feelings of the man with whom she shared it. They were dresses that spoke clearly of personal pride and whispered of secret promises exchanged in private—which was initially why in Harvey Nichols she had wanted to reject them. And why she now wanted to wear them?

Giselle looked at them assessingly. One of them was a fluid handful of dark green jersey, with long sleeves and a boat-shaped neckline, and a floor-length skirt ruched slightly at the sides. The other was black, again with long sleeves, and had a scooped-out back that looked as though it dipped right down to the waist. The fabric was a sheer black silk, over a skintone underskirt.

Of the two, Giselle felt that she would be more comfortable in the green jersey. She looked at her watch. She hadn't got time to dither.

Twenty minutes later she was standing in front of the mirror in the dressing room staring at her own reflection. The dress fitted perfectly, and the colour was unexpectedly flattering for her skin tone, giving it a soft luminous sheen. Theoretically she was covered from her throat through to her wrists and her ankles by the jersey fabric, but somehow—unless she was deceiving herself because it was what she wanted to believe—the dress still managed to be extraordinary and very subtly sexy.

There was a knock at the door and this time it *was* Saul, wearing a dinner suit and looking so very male and handsome that her heart literally somersaulted inside her chest wall as she contrasted the formality of the way he looked now with the intimacy of how she had seen him earlier. And how she wanted to see him later? Her heart somersaulted again.

'I'm not quite ready, I'm afraid. I just need to brush my hair,' she told him, trying to sound calm as he stepped past her and into the room.

'Leave it. It suits you the way it is,' he told her.

Giselle looked at him with suspicion. She'd seen for herself that tendrils of hair had escaped from the clip she'd put in it, and were now curling softly onto her throat and the back of her neck.

'It's untidy,' she protested. 'It looks as though—' She stopped abruptly, realising that she had been about to say that it looked as though she had just got out of bed.

'It looks fine,' Saul insisted, adding, 'besides, we haven't got much time. Don't worry, though. I can promise you that Aldo won't notice. He won't have eyes for anyone other than Natasha, poor fool. Speaking of Natasha, though, I thought you might like to wear these.'

As he spoke Saul was reaching into his pocket and removing a dazzling diamond necklace and a pair of diamond stud earrings.

'They belonged to my mother,' Saul added.

'Your mother?' Giselle shook her head. 'Oh, no—I couldn't possibly wear them.'

'She'd want you to.' As he spoke, Saul recognised to his own surprise that it was the truth. His mother would have liked Giselle. 'You should wear them. Knowing Natasha, she'll be decked out like a Christmas tree.'

'She is,' Giselle agreed absently.

'You've seen her?' Saul queried.

'She came to see me. She wanted to warn me that

you would never commit to me or allow me to have your child. She said you couldn't bear the thought of your son taking second place to Aldo's.'

'It's true that I never intend to have children, but that decision doesn't have anything to do with them not inheriting the dukedom. Let me put this on for you—the catch is a bit awkward,' he told Giselle placing the diamond necklace round her neck before she could stop him.

In the mirror she could see the diamonds sparkling, and Saul standing behind her, his hands on the necklace's clasp. She didn't need to see him, though, to be aware of his presence. She could feel it with every cell of her body. She could feel too his breath on her skin, making her nerve-endings tingle, making her want to turn round and beg him to hold her and kiss her, making her ache to be back where they had been before Aldo's phone call had interrupted them.

Just thinking such thoughts was enough to have the female pulse buried deep inside her quickening into an aching urgency, her senses craving a renewal of that intimacy with him.

'So, if it isn't because they won't inherit the dukedom, then why don't you want children?' she asked, in an attempt to distract herself from her physical awareness of his proximity.

'It isn't a matter of not wanting them so much as a matter of knowing myself and knowing that my work means they would have to take second place in my life—just as my mother's work meant that I had to take second place in hers.'

Saul had finished fastening the necklace, but he didn't

move away from her. He was opening up to her in a way she had not expected, and his words touched her own emotions in a way that both made her ache with longing to comfort him and at the same time filled her with fear *because* she felt that way.

Giselle's silence, as opposed to more questions or a demand for further explanation, had Saul continuing grimly, 'What I learned from that experience taught me that a child deserves to be number one on its parents' list of priorities. My commitments and lifestyle mean that I can't guarantee I'll always be there for my child when he or she needs me. In my opinion it's kinder not to have children at all than to inflict that on them. And as for coveting the dukedom, if that is what Natasha tried to imply, Aldo's title and the responsibilities that go with it—such as the duty to provide an heir, as he must—are the very last thing I would want.'

He paused and then, as though the words were being dragged from him without him being able to control them, he told her, 'My parents could not be there for me when I needed them to be. I will not inflict that on a new generation. My mother used to say to me that I was very fortunate, and that I should not begrudge the time she gave to the children she was trying to help because I had so much. And I didn't begrudge it—I'm very proud of the work she did for those children who had nothing. But she couldn't understand that sometimes a child needs its parents, and I craved to see more of her. I will not father children who will—'

'Be hurt as you were hurt, because they have to come second?' Giselle finished for him.

She ached so much to hold him and be held by him

as she told him that she too knew that pain, that feeling of being pushed to one side, even if in her case it had been by only one child—her baby brother.

'Yes.' Saul's voice was terse. He had said too much, given away too much, and instinctively he wanted to pull back and distance himself both from his vulnerability and from Giselle herself

As a result he was short and sharp. 'Can you manage the earrings yourself?'

Giselle nodded her head.

She could sense that Saul was withdrawing from her, and she understood why. What he had told her had given her much to think about, though. She knew that Saul meant what he had said. She had heard it in his voice and seen it in his expression—and she, of course, understood why he felt the way he did as another woman might not have done. Because of her own experience. It formed a bond between them. But it was a bond that she suspected Saul did not want. And she did? How could she answer that question honestly when she knew the answer she ought to give was not the one that was in her heart.

'Ready?' Saul asked, after she had finished securing the earrings.

'Yes,' Giselle answered him.

'Ah, there you are, you two.'

Aldo might have his height, and something of his looks, but looking at Aldo was like comparing a pale shadow to the reality of all that Saul was, Giselle recognised as Saul introduced her to his cousin.

They were served pre-dinner drinks in the red drawing room, its decor a perfect backdrop for Natasha's

gown and jewels, and then dinner in an even more
formal dining room.

Giselle witnessed the genuine affection Saul felt for
his cousin, and Aldo's reciprocal love and respect for
Saul.

Eventually they were seated in the white drawing
room, and Natasha, who had been drinking steadily all
evening, became truculent as she complained about the
lack of social life in Arezzio.

It was gone midnight, but Giselle wasn't tired. Instead
she was strung up with nervous tension. All evening
there had been only one thing on her mind. One thing.
One end result. But oh, so many sensual diversions she
might take to reach that end result if only Saul would
let her.

She had made up her mind to stop fighting what she
felt, to stop trying to deny herself the satisfaction she
craved. Why shouldn't she for once taste the pleasures
that other women her age took for granted? There could
never be a more perfect man or a more perfect situation
than there was here and now with Saul, who rejected the
idea of commitment and children every bit as fiercely
as she did herself—albeit for different reasons. If Saul
wanted to satisfy the desire he had already aroused in
her there was no reason for her to want to stop him.
Maybe this was even meant to be. Her one chance to
know what it truly meant to be a woman. Fate taking
pity on her and giving her what she had denied herself.
If Saul wanted it to happen.

How did a woman let a man know that she wanted
him without risking humiliating herself if he did not
want her? She had spent so long deliberately making

sure that she did *not* encourage male advances that she did not know how to encourage them. Previously Saul had kissed her in anger. Did that mean that if she made him angry again it would lead to a resurgence of the passion he had shown her earlier?

Saul glanced discreetly at his watch.

'I think it's time Giselle and I called it a night,' he informed Aldo and Natasha, standing up and looking enquiringly at Giselle as he did so.

Obediently Giselle stood up as well, exchanging goodnights with her host and hostess before walking with Saul to the corridor that led to his apartment.

When they reached her bedroom door, Saul told her brusquely, 'I'll say goodnight here.'

Immediately Giselle's heart sank.

'But what about the necklace and the earrings?' she protested.

'You can give them to me in the morning.'

'I don't think I'll be able to unfasten the necklace.'

'Then sleep with it on.'

Saul's voice was sharp now as he stepped back from her. Another few seconds and he would be gone. Desperation filled her.

'I'd rather...' *I'd rather sleep with you.* She had been about to say it, driven to boldness by her need, but Saul didn't let her finish.

Shaking his head, he told her thickly, 'Giselle, just leave it, will you? Because if you don't...' He paused and then said grimly, 'If I go into that room with you, if I touch you, then I warn you that I won't stop touching you until you are lying naked underneath me and I've got you crying out to me in need.'

His voice became muffled as Giselle moved shakily towards him and put her hands on his shoulders. 'And in ecstasy,' he said, and Giselle shuddered wildly as he finished, 'And in the small death that comes from fulfilment.'

'Don't tell me,' she whispered boldly against his mouth. 'Show me.'

Opening the door, Saul swept her up into his arms, kissing her fiercely as he kicked the door shut behind them and carried her over to the bed.

Before he had placed her on it Giselle had slid her hands inside his jacket and started to unfasten his shirt, greedy for the sight and the scent and the feel of him.

As he kissed her, his tongue probing the soft welcome of her mouth, feeling her own tongue twining with his, Saul unzipped her dress, tugging it free of her body, deepening his kiss, passion surging through him as he cupped her breasts.

'The necklace,' Giselle reminded him, reaching behind her neck for the fastening.

'Leave it,' he answered her. 'It suits you.'

The glitter of the diamonds against her naked skin gave her a look of almost pagan sensuality, and made him feel— What? That he had claimed her and set his mark on her? Made her his just as she had made him a prisoner of his desire for her?

He sat up in the bed, intending to remove his jacket and shirt, but Giselle shook her head to stop him, insisting, 'No, let me. I want to do it.'

Saul supposed he must have been undressed by a woman before, but if so he couldn't remember it, and he certainly couldn't remember anything ever being as intoxicatingly erotic as the absorbed concentration of Giselle's gaze on his body, the increasingly rapid, shallow sounds of her breathing, which lifted her breasts as she removed his jacket and her fingers found the buttons on his shirt and unfastened them.

'I want you to lie down.'

Obediently he did as she commanded, caught on a savagely sweet surge of sensual delight when she straddled his hips, leaning over him as she placed her hands on his shoulders, cupping the ball joints of his shoulders, stroking her hands over them and then back again, and then down his arms, closing her eyes and shuddering in a mute delight that he could see reflected in her own flesh as her nipples flared into even more swollen arousal.

Automatically he gripped her hips and then slid his own hands up over her body, but she stopped him, her expression determined and serious as she told him, 'I can't concentrate if you do that, and I want to know every bit of you—how you feel, how you smell, how you taste. I want to know it all.'

There had never been a woman like this one, nor a feeling like the one she was arousing within him, a need like the need raging through him. He slid his hands up and reached for her.

When she bent over him to taste the flesh of his throat Saul wrapped her hair round his hand. He wanted all of her, right here, right now. He wanted to spread her legs and lift her over him and onto him and feel her taking him into her.

Her tongue flicked against his Adam's apple. Saul groaned and arched up against her mouth, begging, 'Stop tormenting me.'

'You're the one tormenting me.'

Her admission was no sooner made than Saul was drawing her down against him, sweeping the dress from her hips, holding her and kissing her and inflaming her senses so much that she didn't even realise that he had undressed himself until he brought her down against himself and she discovered that where there had been fabric there was now hard, bare male flesh.

Spread out on top of him, Giselle could feel the thick hardness of his erection pressing against her thigh. Saul's hands reached down to caress the inside of her parted legs, causing wet heat to explode inside her. His hands moved up and around, cupping her buttocks, then lifting her hips as he slid her up his torso until he could take the eager peak of her nipple into his mouth.

Was this pleasure or was it torture?

She was so wet and eager. Saul could feel her juices dampening his own flesh. His tongue flicked against her nipple, her sharp cry of longing feeding his own arousal. He rolled her over onto her back, his desire fed by her helpless arch towards him as she offered herself to him. He kissed her mouth, cupping her face so that he could take his fill of the sweet pleasure of kissing her, and feeling her body tremble helplessly beneath the lash of her need. Her sex was swollen, opening to the stroke of his hand and his fingers like a rare flower, spreading its petals for him, swelling and trembling wildly beneath his touch. Inside his head he could already taste her sweetness against his tongue, the softly musky scent of her invading his senses.

Giselle wanted to touch Saul as intimately as he was touching her. She wanted to know him and feel him and taste him. She wanted to caress the length and breadth of him with her hands and her lips.

She only knew that she had voiced those desires out loud in a sobbed litany of longing when she heard Saul groan that she was tormenting him beyond reason. And then her plea was answered, so that she could breathe in the most intimate scent of him and answer the aching female need within herself to know his scent and taste whilst he stroked and caressed her so intimately that she could scarcely bear the pleasure of it.

She was hot and wet, and the touch of her hand and her mouth against his sex was driving him to a frenzy of longing that demanded the ultimate satisfaction.

Momentarily bereft of Saul's touch and her contact with his body, Giselle cried out in protest. But it was a very different kind of cry that burst from her lips when he filled her with the firm, deliberate thrust of his body. Her legs wrapped round him, and she gasped out her pleasure in a delirious rush of breath.

Never had any woman held and caressed him so shockingly seductively, making him ache helplessly for the sweet, passionate movement of her muscles as she moved with him.

And then Saul felt it—the unfamiliar but instantly recognisable tightness, the swift tension in her body, the intake of breath. All of them relaying to him the unimaginable and unwanted truth of her virginity.

Saul knew. Giselle could tell. She could feel his attempt to withdraw from her but her body fought it, fiercely defending its need for the pleasure it had been promised. Her muscles wrapped protestingly around him as she gripped his shoulders and rose with him.

'No,' she told him. 'I can't bear it if you stop now. Please don't.'

It was her honesty that undermined him. That and the ache of her open need for him, the first and the only man to whom she had given herself. The full power of his own answering need for her was reignited within him. He hadn't expected or been prepared for the almost atavistic sense of male superiority that filled his body because he knew that hers had singled him out amongst all men to share this pleasure.

He hadn't intended to give in on a logical basis, even if she *had* told him so firmly, 'It's all right, I am on the pill.' There were still questions he needed and wanted to ask, after all. But she was moving against him, opening herself to him, Saul recognised on a shock of fiercely male arousal, taking him deeper, and his body took over from her, filling her, driving her pleasure and his own until they were moving as one, locked together, two bodies, maybe, but with one single goal that they were climbing towards together.

Giselle reached it first, crying out. He felt her body tighten and then expand around him in a succession of explosive movements that brought his own release in a series of hot, pulsing expulsions.

It had happened, Giselle thought gratefully, held in Saul's arms, her head resting on his still damp, thudding chest in weak post-orgasm euphoria and relief. She now knew all there was to know—had experienced the increasing intensity of each individual caress and pleasure there was to experience. She had crossed the barrier into true womanhood and was now complete, fulfilled, replete with the rich satisfaction to which Saul had taken her and then shared with her.

'I wanted it to happen.'

Saul could feel and hear her soft words, reverberating against his flesh, feel their echo striking into his heart and his emotions.

'I wanted it to happen and I wanted you.'

Giselle had no idea why she felt so impelled to say such words. They were not a defence, or even a justification, she needed neither of those. They were more a statement of reaffirmation, a proud simple declaration of her joy, and her belief in the rightness of what had happened. She had touched the heights and she would have that knowledge, that memory for ever to warm her through the cold darkness of the road that lay ahead. Somehow she had found the courage to take the gift fate had handed her in the shape of Saul a man who did not want either commitment from her or children. Yes she had touched the heights and now there was nowhere left for her to go other than to fall from them, but she must not think about that now.

It was later whilst they were showering together, Saul's knowing sensual touch on her body like hearing echoes of music from the most magnificent composer played by the world's best orchestra, singing in the most heavenly way inside her head, that Giselle touched him too. Quickly she lost herself in the delicious pleasure the freedom to touch him so intimately gave her, her concentration so absolute and intent, her gaze so filled with awed delight—like a child discovering that Father Christmas had appeared magically in the night and not only left every gift they could have wanted but also gifts they had never imagined wanting but which they now discovered were exactly what they would have wanted had they been able to think of them.

No woman had looked at him, touched him, wanted him as Giselle did, and watching her filled Saul with a sensation inside as if something hard and implacable in his chest had become a heavy, unwanted weight that was now cracking apart and dissolving, so that where there had been grimness and steel casing there was now lightness and the most ridiculous effervescent fountaining of happiness.

Hugging the towel which Saul had wrapped tenderly around her, Giselle sat on a stool in the ultra-modern grey, black and white kitchen of his royal apartment whilst Saul cooked Eggs Benedict for her. He had ruefully agreed to make her tea when she had shaken her head to the champagne he had originally offered her.

It was gone two o'clock in the morning, but Giselle had never felt more wide awake or more alive.

Sitting with Saul whilst he fed her forkfuls of delicious food, relishing every second of the equally delicious intimacy she was sharing with him, when he asked her the question she had been expecting she was ready for it, and relaxed enough to answer.

'You were a virgin,' he said quietly, followed by, even softer voiced, 'Why did you choose to lose your virginity with me?'

He had put the plate from which he had been feeding her down, and it gave Giselle a small pang of emotion that she hastily pushed away when Saul pulled her to him whilst he waited for her answer, settling her head comfortably against his shoulder. Thank goodness she already knew that this intimacy they were sharing now was no more than a sexually experienced man's way of showing his appreciation for the sex they had shared. It had nothing to do with anything deeply emotional that might have hinted at the development of a true relationship between them. That awareness helped her to focus on her answer to him, and she responded truthfully.

'You already know. Well, sort of.'

Saul's fingers beneath her chin lifted her face, so that he could look down into it.

'I do?' he questioned.

'Yes,' Giselle confirmed, nodding her head. 'I wanted you. That shocked and frightened me at first. It was relatively easy before I met you not to want anyone. I knew, of course, that I couldn't and mustn't, because I knew—well, I felt it would be wrong of me because of—'

'Because of your childhood?'

'Yes,' Giselle agreed, grateful to him for helping her over the stumbling block with which she had been struggling. 'Yes—exactly because of that. I knew I couldn't…I knew I *mustn't* have a child…children. I didn't want to be promiscuous and have a procession of men through my life and my bed, and besides I was afraid that I might start to care for one of them, or they for me, but with you it was different.'

'Because you knew that I would understand your childhood?'

'Yeees…'

Giselle hoped that Saul wouldn't hear the small hesitation in her confirmation and question her more deeply.

She couldn't tell him the deepest and darkest secret that separated her from the fulfilment and happiness other women were free to want—not now when she was so happy, when she felt so complete, and so…so normal. Telling him the truth would only spoil things, and there was no point. No point and no need for him to know, given that she knew this glorious, heavenly, wonderful gift from fate was simply a magical moment out of time, whose beauty, like a delicate soap bubble, could not exist for very long.

The truth was shocking, destructive and ugly. Were she to tell it to him he would look at her so very differently than he was doing now. It wasn't really wrong of her to want to keep these moments precious and safe, was it? Not when his knowing was so unnecessary, and when she already knew that the pleasure he had given her was quite literally all she could have of him.

Poor child. She must have suffered even more than *he* had because of the loss of her parents. And not just her parents, he remembered, there had been a small child involved as well—a baby sibling. Knowing that child had lost its life was bound to have created in her young mind an awareness of the fragility of human life and a fear of losing those she loved.

Saul drew her even closer, filled with tenderness for her and a desire to protect her—things he would once have repudiated with anger immediately had he thought he might experience them, but which now, instead of being his hated enemies, seemed natural and necessary accompaniments to the other emotions he was feeling. Emotions? He would question his own feelings later, Saul told himself. Right now his duty of care was for

Giselle. For the child she had once been when he had not been there to protect her, and for the woman she had become in his arms now that he was. Such a huge step could not be taken without the person taking it being deeply affected by it, even if Giselle herself was not aware of that fact yet. He was aware of it, and it was up to him to see to it that she made that transition safely.

'I was so afraid and angry when I realised that I wanted you, but then I kept hearing about your views on…on things.'

Saul knew she meant on his not wanting a child, and he bent to kiss the top of her head.

'Today—I mean yesterday, when we arrived,' Giselle corrected herself, squirming in heady pleasure as Saul kissed the side of her neck, his hand finding her willing breast beneath the wrappings of her towel and caressing it softly whilst she talked. 'When you kissed me and everything I wanted you so much.' She looked up at him. 'I'd wanted you before, and wanting you had kept me awake at night, thinking and imagining. I knew I couldn't bear not to know, to spend the rest of my life wishing. I felt at first that fate was tempting me and tormenting me—laughing at me because I couldn't be with you. But then I thought perhaps fate was really trying to *give* me something, to make it up to me, and that I should…if you wanted to. And then tonight, when you didn't want to come into my bedroom with me, I felt so desperate.'

'I didn't want to because I knew what would happen if I did,' Saul told her.

'And now that it has, do you regret it?' Giselle asked him anxiously.

'Do you?' Saul pushed the question back to her.

'No,' Giselle answered him, simply and truthfully.

'Good,' Saul told her, without answering her question himself, and pulling her to him he kissed her until nothing else mattered.

Somehow they made it back to the bedroom—his this time because, as he told her explicitly in between increasingly intimate caresses, it was closer than hers, and he was close to not making it as far as *any* bed, thanks to the way she was kissing him and touching him.

His bedroom, like the kitchen, was decorated in masculine shades of off-white, grey and black, with just a softening touch of dark cream.

Saul slammed the bedroom door and reached for her, leaning her back against it as he lifted her so that she could wrap her legs eagerly around him. His sex, almost of its own volition, was nudging its way between the lips of her sex, to rub eagerly against her slick readiness and then hotly and eagerly to move within her, filling her so wholly and completely that her body sang with joy.

This time there was no restriction and no hesitation. Her womanhood rejoiced in the full hard presence of him and embraced him, holding him, urging him to move ever deeper and faster.

Her orgasm was swift and intense, driving the breath from her lungs so that she couldn't even cry out her pleasure. Saul cried out his, though, in a deep shout of exultation as Giselle's body took the gift of his release from him and his body pumped its pleasure into her soft, warm readiness.

Another shower, with Giselle almost falling asleep

beneath it this time, and then they were back in bed. She was asleep as soon as her head touched the pillow.

Saul didn't sleep, though. Instead he propped his head up on his hand, his elbow on the pillow, and watched her, frowning as he did so.

What was happening to him? He didn't know. He only knew that tonight something profound and deep-rooted within him had been shaken to its core; beliefs he had thought set in stone had been revealed as shaky because the foundations had been split along a fault line that tonight had exposed.

He felt vulnerable, he recognised, like a creature robbed of its protective shell. It was only sex, he told himself. That was all. Just sex. And, no matter how fundamental its effect on him might be now, it did not and could not change anything about the way he intended to live his life. What had happened between them was just a one-off, an event out of time. It meant nothing to him other than that. And besides, it was Aldo he should be thinking about—not himself, and certainly not Giselle.

The discussions he had had with his cousin had shown him that the situation was even worse than he had first suspected. Aldo hadn't just invested his own money, or rather the money Saul had given him, in the fraudulent investment scheme with its far too high interest rates—which would have alerted anyone who understood the financial world better to the fact that it had to be a con—he had also invested the state's money in it. Money which was needed to pay for teachers and nurses and doctors, and to run public services and infrastructures.

When Saul had asked Aldo why he had said nothing to him prior to making these investments, why he had not sought his advice, Aldo had replied shamefacedly that he had been told not to discuss the scheme with anyone, because access to it was limited to only a few specially chosen investors.

'Natasha felt that if you knew you would want to invest in it as well. Please do not blame her,' Aldo had begged him. 'The fault is entirely mine. Natasha's only fault was that out of her love for me she wanted to prove to you that we could be independent of your generosity. She has far more pride than I do, Saul, and she feels that since I am Grand Duke, I should be…'

'Richer than me?' Saul had supplied wryly, but he had known that what his cousin did not want to say was that Natasha wanted her husband to take precedence over him in every single way—because she felt that that would punish him for not wanting her.

Right now, though, saving his cousin from the public embarrassment of being declared bankrupt, and the knock-on effect that would have on the country and its finances, was far more important to him than Natasha's spitefulness.

He mentally reviewed his own assets to assess which of them he could most readily and easily realise in order to refloat Aldo's finances.

It was perhaps a pity he had bought the island, but having done so he wasn't prepared to sell it at a loss. There were other assets he could sell, though, such as his share in a new office block in Singapore. Aldo was family, and sometimes family had to come first.

CHAPTER TEN

GISELLE had woken up once already, to find that she was pinned to the bed by the weight of Saul's leg lying across her lower body and his arm holding her against his side. It was a welcome imprisonment, though, and it enabled her to lie silently within its captivity and marvel at the magical events of the night and the happiness they had brought her. Now she was awake again—this time to find that she had the bed—his bed—to herself, and that she could stretch out languorously in it, entranced by the sweetly heavy ennui that possessed her body as intimately and intensely as Saul had possessed it during the night.

Saul *was* her perfect lover, in every single way. With him there was no need for her to feel guilt because of the pain she might ultimately cause him, or to fear her own emotions. She knew that this pleasure that filled her and surrounded her like a fluffy pink cloud of delight was only fleeting and could only be enjoyed very briefly. And if knowing that brought safety, perhaps it also heightened its sweetness—because she knew it could only be for now, for this short precious time beyond which she was not going to look until she had to.

Their time together, like the intimacy it had brought,

could not continue once they returned to London. That would be impossible. She knew that. There was no need for Saul to say so to her, and she hoped that he believed her and trusted her enough to know that. She didn't want a single second of this special time spoiled or marred by any kind of discord or distrust between them.

How she would deal with the realities of life once they were back in London she would figure out once she was back there. If Saul chose to end her secondment to him then so be it. It would be the sensible and practical action to take—and that sharp, agonised fluttering of anguish inside her chest was simply a knee-jerk reaction and didn't actually mean anything, she assured herself firmly. Nevertheless, it was enough to have her getting out of bed and making her way to her own bedroom, where she showered and dressed in one of the tee shirts and the skirt that her personal shopper had recommended to her.

It wasn't because last night Saul had stroked his hand along the length of her leg and said how long and slender her legs were that she was wearing a skirt instead of trousers or jeans. It was simply because she could see that outside the sun was shining. It was spring, the trees were in blossom, and a light skirt seemed more appropriate than something heavy.

Saul, already showered and dressed when he had kissed her awake earlier, had told her that they would have to stay in Arezzio for longer than he had originally planned because of the complexity of his cousin's financial affairs. Giselle had hugged that news to herself, gloating like a miser given a pure gold coin over the prospect of their intimacy being extended.

She was just brushing her hair when a messenger arrived in the form of a maid dressed in black, her brown hair coiled round her head in plaits. She looked young and nervous, Giselle could see, immediately feeling sorry for her as she bobbed a small curtsy and informed her that the Grand Duchess had sent her, to see if Giselle would like to accompany her on a shopping trip into the city.

Accompanying Natasha anywhere was the last thing Giselle felt like doing. But good manners compelled her to accept the other woman's invitation and to follow the maid back along the now more familiar corridors and down the flights of stairs until she was standing in a sunshine-filled room decorated in shades of lemon and powder-blue, where Natasha was seated on a gold-brocade-covered sofa.

'Ah, there you are,' she greeted Giselle, flicking a dismissive gaze over her before smoothing her hand over what Giselle knew must be an infinitely superior and far more expensive designer outfit of golden-yellow silk. The skirt of her dress was so short and tight that Giselle was surprised she was able to sit down in it—to sit down in it *and* then walk in the vertiginous strappy white leather metal-studded heels she was wearing.

Heavy diamond-encrusted bracelets circled her narrow wrists, and her make-up, if anything, was even more heavy than it had been the night before.

'A business associate of my father has opened a shop here in the city, and this morning he has telephoned me to say that he has in some clothes by a new designer that he knows I will love.'

* * *

It was late afternoon. The shopping trip had not been a success, at least as far as Giselle was concerned. Natasha had spent her time flirting with the odiously oily friend of her father, who had encouraged her to try on and then parade in front of him in a selection of increasingly short and tight-fitting outfits, each one of which had seemed to require that he tugged and pulled at the fabric, whilst leering at Natasha in a way that had turned Giselle's stomach and aroused her indignation and pity on Aldo's behalf. Poor Aldo. The outfits Natasha had tried on were surely more suited to a Page Three model desperate for attention than to a Grand Duchess, but of course it had not been Giselle's place to say so.

On their return to the palace Aldo had been so genuinely pleased that Natasha had had the chance to spend time with an old friend that Giselle had felt like asking Natasha if she *knew* how fortunate she was and what she was risking losing with her contempt for Aldo's adoration and love. But then Giselle had reminded herself that she was in no position to lecture anyone about their emotions, or allying sexual desire to those emotions, when she herself was so determined not to do so.

Now the four of them were sitting in the blue and yellow salon, and Aldo was telling her it had been his and Saul's grandmother's favourite room.

'Which is why we always take tea here—because it was her habit to do so.'

Natasha pulled a face when Aldo said this, and insisted that what *she* wanted was a vodka and champagne cocktail—the same cocktail she had been drinking at the dress shop, Giselle knew. And she felt even more sorry for Aldo when his kind face became slightly shadowed. Because Natasha threatened a fuss if she refused, Giselle was also obliged to drink a cocktail instead of the tea she would have preferred.

The alcohol did not seem to be improving Natasha's temper, which now flared up again as Aldo suggested very discreetly that perhaps she already had enough expensive clothes.

'What?' she challenged her husband, before gulping at her drink—her third since they had all sat down. 'So now you mean to deny me the only pleasure I've got left, do you? Since being good in bed isn't exactly your forte, is it, darling? You should perhaps ask Saul for some tips.'

Giselle could hear the sound of Saul's expelled breath as he stood behind her, and no wonder. Poor Aldo must feel mortified—although he was merely shaking his head and saying gently, 'I think you are embarrassing our guest a little, Natasha.'

'Is that possible?' Natasha retaliated. 'Can *anyone* embarrass one of Saul's women? I wouldn't have thought so.'

Giselle suspected that Natasha's drinking had brought her mood to that borderline where it could easily move from mere truculence to something more unpleasant. For Aldo's sake she didn't want to provoke her into crossing that line, even though her stomach muscles had tightened defensively with dislike for her.

Rather than retaliate, she decided to make her exit, and said quietly, avoiding looking at anyone, 'I'm feeling rather tired. If you will excuse me, I think I'll go to my room.'

'I'll come with you,' Saul said immediately. 'I've got some work to do myself.'

'I'm sorry about that,' Saul apologised the minute they were on their own. 'Natasha's behaviour was appalling. I don't know how Aldo puts up with her.

'He loves her, and he's afraid of losing her,' Giselle assessed as he unlocked the door that led to his private apartment and held it open for her.

'I feel desperately sorry for any child they end up having… I think that Natasha will be a very demanding mother, with exacting standards for any child they have, but especially a son. She's so competitive herself that a…a more sensitive child will find it hard to deal with.' He paused, mulling over the way she had behaved. 'If you were to ask me, I would say that there's a degree of instability within Natasha. I hadn't noticed it before, but today…'

Giselle's mouth had gone dry, and her heart was pounding. 'I think it was just the drink that made her behave the way she did.'

'You're defending her?' Saul's eyebrows rose. 'That's very charitable of you, but I thought her behaviour pointed quite plainly to some kind of emotional and perhaps even mental instability—and that can only lead to a great deal of unhappiness for those close to her.'

Giselle gave a small involuntary shiver, and Saul guessed why immediately.

'You're thinking of your own childhood?'

'Yes,' Giselle was forced to admit. 'I was just thinking how hard it will be for Aldo and Natasha's children.'

'Because Natasha will neglect them emotionally?''

'Yes. And…' She paused, and Saul prompted her.

'And?'

Her voice very low and sad, Giselle told him, 'And because they will have to bear the stigma of being tainted by their mother's emotional instability and the fear that she might have passed it down to them. They will be judged because of that. People always make judgements.'

'You sound as though you speak from personal experience?'

It was too late now to recognise that she had come perilously close to a very dangerous place and to wish she had stayed silent.

'I was judged because of the accident—because I lived and they…they didn't.' She forced herself to admit it. 'By my father and I dare say others.'

'Your father judged you?' Saul stopped walking and turned to her. 'Why should anyone judge you for something over which you had no control? You were a child.'

It was too late to hold back the roaring, rolling tide of her pain now. It was engulfing her and sweeping her up into its shuddering darkness, making her feel like a child again—alone, abandoned, unwanted, *guilty*…

They had reached the bedroom. Saul opened the door, surprising himself with his need to comfort her as he told her firmly, 'You were not to blame. It wasn't your fault.'

It wasn't your fault. She had hungered so much over the years to hear those words spoken to her, to feel that someone knew and understood her pain and wanted to help her. That they wouldn't blame her or turn away from her. That they wouldn't choose death rather than live with her. As her father had done.

She had heard the whispers after his death, murmured behind the hands of well-meaning adults too consumed by their own curiosity and shock to realise that a seven-year-old child was perfectly capable of translating what they were saying when they commented that her father had had a heart attack because he hadn't wanted to live after the deaths of her mother and her baby brother.

She had understood what they were saying. She had understood too why her father had sent her away to live with her great-aunt. It was because he had known the truth. He had always blamed her. He had recognised her guilt and he had left her alone with it and her fear of it.

Her father's desertion of her had hurt her dreadfully and left her feeling that she had been a burden to him that he hadn't wanted. A burden he had only been able to escape via death. She had known then that she must never burden anyone else with her love, just as she could never—

Her body shuddered again, but this time Saul's arms were around her. She didn't want to think about the past—she didn't walk to talk about it or be overshadowed by it. All she wanted was to be in this moment, in Saul's arms. She lifted her face for his kiss.

Saul kissed her, and kept on kissing her whilst he undressed her, and each slither of fabric sliding from her body made her feel as though she was shedding another unwanted layer of inhibition, in doing so setting free the passionate, sensual side of her nature that had for so long been repressed.

Only in Saul's arms, in Saul's bed, did she really feel that she became herself and truly alive, that she reached and touched the true essence of herself. But she knew that her pleasure and its intensity could only be hers for a very short span of time. That meant not wasting a second of it—which was why her hands were urgent in their determination to undress him, as his were to undress her. Their journey towards the pure flesh-on-flesh contact they both craved was broken and delayed by shared kisses and caresses that had soft crooning sounds of pleasure murmuring from Giselle's throat.

Eventually they were free to touch and enjoy one another as they both ached to do. Giselle ran her fingertips the length of Saul's erection and then tried to encircle it with her hand, lifting her awed and aroused gaze to meet the hot intensity of his when his width was too great for her to completely capture it in her hold. She could still caress him, and stroked the slick, hot, pliable flesh that covered the head of his erection with aching longing, feeling the moist heat swell within her own sex, already imagining the moment when his erection would stroke against her aroused and eager flesh, making it flower open for him whilst her muscles quivered in eager anticipation of his first longed-for thrust.

She wouldn't make it to the bed. She couldn't wait that long. But Saul had anticipated her need and they were already on the bed, and he was lying on his back and lifting her over him so that she could take control of her own pleasure.

She wanted desperately to rush and satisfy her hunger, but some age-old female instinct held her back, whispering to her that their shared pleasure would be all the greater for being taken slowly.

And that instinct was right. To look into Saul's eyes as she took him slowly into her, seeing how helpless he was in the face of his desire and her control of it, watching the longing and need he couldn't hide from her as she moved down a little on him, and then stopped to rise up again, brought her such a rush of pleasure that it was almost as though she had orgasmed already.

Her flesh quickened around Saul's, her own hunger overpowering her desire to draw out their shared pleasure and make it last. Saul's hands gripped her hips, holding her as he moved her up and down over his aroused flesh, slowly and deliberately, until the pleasure became a form of torment as she begged for more—deeper, harder.

'Like this, you mean?' he demanded, teasing her with a slower movement. 'Or like this?' He was holding her down on him now, thrusting fiercely and deeply into her, and the raw pleasure of it was making her cry out to him that she couldn't bear it, and not to stop.

And he didn't—not even when she orgasmed. He took her through it, carrying her on upwards whilst her body collapsed and clung, and she was wrung with orgasm after orgasm until finally he took the last of her pleasure from her and filled her with his own release.

Too exhausted to move, Giselle lay against his body as an unwanted realisation washed over her. She was in love with Saul. Panic exploded inside her. No. That mustn't happen. She mustn't love Saul. The most terrible

pain was gripping her—the pain of having a protective
veil ripped from her to reveal the edges of a wound that
went so deep she knew she hadn't even begun to feel its
real pain yet.

She loved Saul. *No!* Yes, she did. Of course she did.
And he wanted her. Wanted her—that was all. This
intimacy between them wouldn't and couldn't last, but
for now he was here, and for now she could and would
give thanks for that.

'I'm going to put on weight if we keep doing this,'
Giselle mock-complained to Saul three hours later, as
she sat up in bed greedily eating the smoked salmon and
cream cheese bagels he had brought her when they'd
realised they had well and truly missed dinner.

'Mmm? Then I'll have to come up with a way of
making sure that you work it off,' Saul teased her.

He had been thinking about her all the time they'd
been apart earlier in the day, longing impatiently to be
with her—something he had never experienced before.
That alone should have been enough to worry him, but
strangely when he was with Giselle all he seemed able
to think about was her. There'd be time enough when
they returned to London for him to put things in their
proper perspective and to end what should never really
have begun.

But it *had* begun, and was he absolutely sure that he
could end it? Of course he was. Commitment wasn't on
his agenda. But then neither had Giselle herself been on
his agenda when they had first met. That was different,
Saul told himself impatiently. Commitment and Giselle

went into different compartments in his life. So why was he thinking about them together?

Saul removed the plate from the bed, and then reached for Giselle's hand, drawing her close to him.

CHAPTER ELEVEN

THEY were returning to London this afternoon, Saul having cancelled their visit to the island because he needed to set up some meetings with regard to Aldo's financial affairs. Now, this morning, Giselle was exploring the old city in the May sunshine and trying to tell herself that she would be able to find the strength to live without Saul in her life. She knew she would have to.

She had it all planned. When he told her it was over, she was going to give in her notice and put her flat up for sale. She would buy a small house in Yorkshire and then she could look after her great-aunt herself. Far away from London and looking after her great-aunt she wouldn't be able to weaken and make a fool of herself by begging Saul to take her back to his bed. Because she had fallen in love with him. Despair shuddered through her. How easily she had given in to temptation and broken her self-imposed rules. But all was not lost. Saul did not love her. They would part. She could still keep the promise she had made to herself.

The narrow streets of the old town twisted and turned, the upper windows of the old medieval three- and four-storey houses almost touching one another across them. Some of them were built into the city walls, and others clung to a jumble of alleyways, their black and white façades stooping beneath the weight of their heavy slate roofs.

Saul couldn't concentrate on the complex financial data on the computer screen in front of him. He couldn't concentrate on anything other than Giselle, he recognised grimly. And that meant…? It meant nothing other than that for now he wanted her in his life and his bed. For now. Until they both agreed that whatever was currently burning in them was reduced to ashes and they were free to go their separate ways.

He tried to go back to his work, but the ache inside him refused to be ignored. He wanted to be with Giselle. He knew she was spending the morning exploring the old city. He wanted to be with her. Not just in bed with her, but *with* her. He wanted to see her expression as she explored his home city. He wanted to see it through her eyes. He wanted…

Cursing beneath his breath, he switched off his laptop and stood up. It shouldn't be hard to find her. The old city wasn't very large, and he knew every single winding inch of its narrow streets.

Once he was outside he started to walk briskly, and then more swiftly as the urgency within him grew.

When he finally saw her she was half the length of a street away from him, poised on the pavement of one of the busier streets, just where it opened out into the town square. She was standing completely still, her gaze apparently fixed on the opposite side of the road. At first Saul thought she must be waiting to cross it, and then he realised that she was watching a young mother who was trying to cope with a buggy with a baby in it and an impatient toddler, who was trying to push the buggy and refusing to take her hand.

Saul started to make his way towards her.

Giselle had seen the young mother with her two children as she herself was just about to cross the unexpectedly busy road, with traffic moving at speed, full-pelt towards the square.

The little boy had grabbed the handle of the buggy and was trying to push it, whilst his harassed mother remonstrated with him, insisting that he hold her hand. Giselle knew the words she would be saying—after all, they were engraved on her own heart, in her own mother's voice.

'Hold on to the pram. Hold my hand. Don't let go. Don't pull. Don't...'

The child was trying to pull free of his mother's hand. She turned away from the buggy to remonstrate with him for another minute, and...

Careless of her own safety, Giselle plunged into the seething traffic, oblivious to the sound of car horns and the warning shouts of drivers, only one thought in her mind as time swung backwards for her and she stepped through its open door into her own past.

She must save them. She must save all of them—not just herself.

What was Giselle doing, running blindly into the traffic like that? She was going to be killed.

Saul reacted automatically, driven by the greatest fear known to man—that of losing that which they loved above all things. He barely registered what his own reaction meant as he plunged after her, covering the distance with superhuman speed, snatching her almost from beneath the wheels of an oncoming car and dragging her to the safety of the pavement.

'What were you doing? Trying to kill yourself?'

Giselle could feel the angry thud of Saul's heart against her own chest. She could hear the voices of the concerned onlookers who had seen what had happened and were now pressing in on them to ask if she was all right. But those things were at a distance from her. All she could think of, all she could ask was, 'The buggy—the baby…is it all right?'

Saul looked down into her pale tense face, and then glanced across the road.

'All three of them are fine,' he told her truthfully.

All three of them. All three of them, but not all three of her family. Not all three of *them.* They had not been fine. She had saved herself, but she had let her mother and her baby brother die. She had sent them to their deaths. She had…

A terrible dry sob tore at her throat.

'I killed them. It was my fault. I shouldn't have let go of the pram. I should have saved them or died with them.' She was not looking at him, Saul saw, his heart turning over inside his chest, but past him.

'Giselle?'

Immediately she focused on him.

'I'm sorry,' she told him politely—as politely as though he was a stranger, he recognized.

Suddenly he was desperate to make her look at him and be with him—to make her… To make her what? Recognise what *he* had just recognised when he had feared that he might lose her, and to tell him as he wanted to tell her that she was his life and he never wanted to let her out of his sight again? Was this love? This feeling that a part of you lay open and bleeding with a wound that could only be healed by complete fusion with another person, a special person, one's perfect other half? If it was, no wonder he had feared it. It was so huge, so all-encompassing, so fearsome, that any human could be forgiven for trembling when confronted by its might. He wanted to tell Giselle what he had discovered, but now was not the time when she was so obviously suffering from shock.

'I'm taking you back to the palace,' he told her, 'and then I'm going to call a doctor.'

'No.' Giselle stopped him. 'No. I don't need a doctor. I'm perfectly all right.'

It wasn't true, of course, and she could see from Saul's grim expression that he didn't believe her.

Saul looked across at the bed where Giselle lay, fully dressed and fast asleep. She had been trembling violently and convulsively by the time he had got her back to the palace, and she had made no demur when he had insisted on pouring her a brandy and making her drink it, and had passively acquiesced when he'd suggested that she should lie down and rest.

Her near accident had obviously and naturally shocked her. It had shocked *him*. He could still hear the protesting squeal of the tyres and brakes on the cars that had thankfully managed to avoid hitting her.

On the bed, Giselle moved restlessly in her brandy-induced sleep, a protesting *'No!'* wrenched from her throat, followed by an almost violent movement of her limbs, as though she was trying to run, and then she screamed.

'Mummy, no!'

Her agonized cry was filled with such terror that the sound of it ripped at Saul's heart and took him to his feet. He reached the bed just as she opened her eyes and struggled to sit up.

She had had the nightmare again—the first time for years—and this time it had seemed so real, every detail so clear and sharp. She had even been able to smell the rain mingling with her mother's scent, and then the smell of the blood—blood everywhere—on her clothes and on her hands. She looked down at them and then closed her eyes, agonised tears seeping from them to burn her face in the same way that the acid of her guilt was burning into her soul.

'Giselle?' She felt Saul reach for her and take her in his arms. 'Talk to me,' he commanded. 'Tell me what's wrong.'

Giselle opened her eyes again. She was too weary to fight to protect herself and conceal her guilt any longer. She was going to lose Saul anyway, so what did it matter if she had to look at him and see the disgust in his eyes?

She exhaled in defeat.

'It was the mother—the mother with the buggy and the little boy. They reminded me… I thought…'

Her voice was so low that Saul had to strain to hear what she was saying.

'I should have stopped them. I shouldn't have let go of my mother's hand and the pram. If I hadn't…'

She was talking about her childhood, Saul realised, beginning to understand that in some way seeing that mother with her buggy and her young child must have reminded her of the terrible accident that had robbed her of her own mother and baby brother.

'I should have died with them. That's what my father thought. That's why he sent me away instead of letting me stay with him. He couldn't bear the sight of me because I didn't save them. He knew I should have died with them.'

Saul was appalled.

'No, Giselle,' he assured her, wrapping his arms round her. 'No. That's not true.'

'Yes, it is,' Giselle insisted. 'It was my fault. If I'd held on to them… But I didn't. I pulled away. I let go and they died. Mummy was angry with me because I hadn't wanted to go out. It was dark and raining, but she said we needed to go out because Thomas wouldn't stop crying. She told me to put Thomas in his pram, and then she said that we'd walk to the park and I could go on the swings. But then when we were nearly at the park she changed her mind and said that we were going to cross the road instead. She told me to hold her hand, but I didn't want to. I wanted to go to the park like she had promised. She grabbed hold of my arm, but I pulled free, and then she started to cross the road. I screamed at her to stop because there was a lorry coming, but she wouldn't, and then…and then it was too late. It was my fault they were killed.'

'No.' Saul immediately rejected her guilt, horrified to think of the mental pain and guilt she must have endured. 'No. It was not your fault. It was an accident and you were not to blame.' He smoothed her damp hair back off her face and commanded, 'Look at me.'

Silently Giselle did so.

'Do you really think that fate would have wanted or allowed you to die when she had already promised you to me?'

His words had Giselle's eyes widening.

'What…what do you mean?'

'When I saw you plunge into that traffic and thought that I might lose you I realised the truth. I love you, Giselle. I think I probably fell in love with you in that wretched car park when you stole my parking space and then defied me. Fate brought us together there that day because she meant us to be together.'

'No,' Giselle protested, immediately panicking. 'You can't love me. You mustn't. We mustn't love each other.'

'Because we might be hurt?' Saul leaned his forehead against hers and kissed the bridge of her nose. 'This is why you feel you shouldn't love anyone and why you don't want a child, isn't it? Because of what happened to your mother and baby brother?'

Giselle hesitated. Now was the time to tell him everything. She wanted to. She wanted to desperately. But somehow the words just would not come. She was too afraid to speak them, so instead she nodded her head.

It was after all the truth in its way—even if it was not the whole of that truth. Surely she could have this sweetest of precious times with him? Surely she could have just a little longer before she had to give him up to a woman who would be able to give him what she never could?

'I didn't want you to know. I didn't want you to blame me and look at me the way my father did. I could have saved them, Saul, but I didn't—I let them go,' she told him emotionally.

'No. You think that now, but you were a child—what could you have done?'

He could so easily picture the scene—the dark wet road, the tired mother impatient to get home, her mind on other things, stepping out into the road, expecting the child whose hand she had released to follow her. The thought of what all the years of carrying the guilt she should never have been allowed to carry must have done to her brought a huge lump to his throat and a vow to his heart that he would love her so much that she would never again feel any pain.

'I love you,' he told her, knowing as he said the words that he meant them, and surprised only that he had been foolish enough to fight against the truth for so long with his mind, when his body and his heart had already recognised and given themselves up to their love for Giselle. 'There is nothing you could ever do or be that could stop me loving you,' he said softly. 'Nothing. I want to marry you, Giselle.'

Immediately she stiffened in his hold.

'No. You can't. You can't want to marry me.'

Saul was amused, and teased her. 'Oh, I see—you've got a husband already, have you? Very well, then, that marriage will have to be annulled. After all, you were never properly his—not like you have become my woman, my love, my life,' he told her, his voice thickening as he bent his head to kiss her.

She couldn't resist him any more than she could resist her own need.

'Fate intended us to be together,' Saul insisted firmly. 'I am more sure of that than anything I have been sure of before. For us to meet, for us to love, for us to be together is our mutual and shared destiny.' Every cell within him, inherited from the generations that had gone before, told Saul that. 'Fate even gave us both a messed-up childhood, so that we could understand one another. Out of the cruelty of the loss we have known fate has forged a bond and a bridge for us which we can cross from our separate aloneness to a shared future.'

'Those are lovely words,' Giselle responded. 'But...'

'They are more than words,' Saul assured her. 'They are my promise to you for our future together—and we *will* have a future together, Giselle. What we have together is too special for us not to.'

Every word he spoke was like a knife being driven into her heart. She so much wanted what he was offering her—but how could she trust him to love her as she was, for always?

'Marriage usually means children,' she told him huskily, 'and I can never have your child, Saul. My feelings on that will never change.'

His hand closed round hers.

'Have I said that I want them to? The truth is, Giselle, that I am *glad* that you do not want children. My own feelings on that subject have not changed. You and I, we can travel together, be together, work together. Together we will construct buildings of great beauty, great power and passion wherever we are called upon to do so. We cannot do that, commit wholly to that and to one another, *and* have children. Our creations shall be our progeny, our gift.'

He spoke so eloquently, so believably and so enticingly, that Giselle felt dazzled by the breadth of his vision and the depth of his commitment to her and to their future together.

'Do you promise?' she asked him. 'Do you promise that you mean it, Saul?'

'We don't need children to prove our love for one another. I don't need anything or anyone other than you, Giselle.'

Such emotive, tender words—soothing her hurts, filling her with courage, feeding her own love for him.

'I love you, Giselle.'

'And I love you too.'

There it was—said. A promise asked for and given. A commitment made. A love shared.

Would it be wrong of her to take Saul's love and give him her own? If they didn't have children their love would be safe. He need never know about that... that other thing. He would surely turn away from her in revulsion if he did. But he didn't need to know, did he? she pleaded inwardly with her conscience. If they were destined to be together, as he had said, then she must be destined not to have a child and not to have to tell him.

The temptation was too much for her—especially when he was kissing her as he was right now...

EPILOGUE

THEY were married three months later, in the cathedral in Arezzio, in keeping with Parenti family tradition.

Giselle wore a white Chanel bridal gown. Saul had insisted on her wearing white. Her great-aunt attended the ceremony, and Giselle saw in the old lady's face how happy she was for her.

Natasha, wearing one of her favoured too-short, too-tight dresses, glared at her when she walked back down the aisle on Saul's arm as his wife, but Giselle didn't care. She was too happy, too filled with love and gratitude to feel anything other than pity for Natasha.

Saul had dealt with Aldo's debts and discreetly restored the country's finances to stability. Once they returned from their honeymoon work was going to start on the island, and the new resort was going to be Giselle's personal project—a wedding gift to her from Saul.

Now there was just time for a final few minutes with her great-aunt whilst Saul was with Aldo, before they left on their honeymoon.

'I wish your father was here today to see you so happy, Giselle. He loved you so much.'

'My father *loved* me?' She was too shocked to

hold back the words. 'How could he when he sent me away?'

'Oh, Giselle. He asked me to take you because he felt there were too many sad memories for you in being with him. He wanted you to have a fresh start. He felt so guilty about what had happened—and over your mother.'

'*He* felt guilty? I thought he blamed me.'

'Never.' Her great-aunt shook her head vigorously. 'He blamed himself. He worried that what you had witnessed would scar you, and that being with him would only make that worse. He would have been so proud to see you as you are today. You have married a good man, Giselle, a man who loves you as you deserve to be loved—and I can see that you love him in the same way. That is good. No one should marry for anything less than the very best love there is.' She paused, and then asked gently, 'You have told Saul everything, I expect?'

Giselle couldn't meet her great-aunt's probing look.

'I've told him everything he needs to know,' she replied.

Her great-aunt squeezed Giselle's hand.

'I'm so glad. There should not be secrets between a couple who love one another. Secrets can cause such dreadful damage.'

Saul was coming over. Giselle kissed her great-aunt's cheek, and felt the now familiar quiver of achingly sweet need possess her body as she looked up at her new husband. Surely nothing could spoil her happiness now. Surely now she could finally put the past behind her?

'It's time for us to leave,' Saul told her.

Nodding her head, Giselle gave him her hand—just as she had already given him her heart.

Now, finally, they were on their own—alone together in their bungalow on a luxurious and exclusive resort complex. Their butler had cleared away the remains of their evening meal, they had walked on their private beach and then swum naked together in the moonlight, and now they were celebrating their commitment to one another in the most intimate and private way possible.

Saul was anointing her body with kisses so tender they were almost reverential, and the love they shared was surely as he had told her—meant to be, and strong enough to hold at bay even the darkest of fears. And the guilt? Could that be held at bay too?

It must be. It must be consigned to the past. Because it had no place here in her life with Saul. Nothing could hurt her now that she had his love. Nothing could harm her. She was safe, their love was safe, and she had nothing to fear.

'You are all I want and all I will ever want,' Saul told her, as he had told her when she had committed herself to him. 'Just you, only you, and nothing else.'

She knew he meant it. Surely nothing could spoil things for her now? Surely fate had decided to relent and allow her to be happy? Could she be happy, knowing the secret she was keeping from Saul? *Yes.* Yes, because it couldn't harm either of them now.

'Love me,' she begged Saul, clinging to him with fierce passion. 'Love me, Saul.'

Beneath his answering kiss she offered up a mental

prayer for their happiness, before offering up herself on the altar of their shared love.

Nothing could part them now. Nothing could damage or destroy what they had. *Nothing.*

REQUEST YOUR FREE BOOKS!

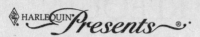

2 FREE NOVELS PLUS
2 FREE GIFTS!

YES! Please send me 2 FREE Harlequin Presents® novels and my 2 FREE gifts (gifts are worth about $10). After receiving them, if I don't wish to receive any more books, I can return the shipping statement marked "cancel." If I don't cancel, I will receive 6 brand-new novels every month and be billed just $4.05 per book in the U.S. or $4.74 per book in Canada. That's a saving of at least 15% off the cover price! It's quite a bargain! Shipping and handling is just 50¢ per book.* I understand that accepting the 2 free books and gifts places me under no obligation to buy anything. I can always return a shipment and cancel at any time. Even if I never buy another book, the two free books and gifts are mine to keep forever.

106/306 HDN E5M4

Name _____ (PLEASE PRINT) _____

Address _____ Apt. #

City _____ State/Prov. _____ Zip/Postal Code

Signature (if under 18, a parent or guardian must sign)

Mail to the Harlequin Reader Service:
IN U.S.A.: P.O. Box 1867, Buffalo, NY 14240-1867
IN CANADA: P.O. Box 609, Fort Erie, Ontario L2A 5X3

Not valid for current subscribers to Harlequin Presents books.

Are you a current subscriber to Harlequin Presents books and want to receive the larger-print edition? Call 1-800-873-8635 today!

* Terms and prices subject to change without notice. Prices do not include applicable taxes. N.Y. residents add applicable sales tax. Canadian residents will be charged applicable provincial taxes and GST. Offer not valid in Quebec. This offer is limited to one order per household. All orders subject to approval. Credit or debit balances in a customer's account(s) may be offset by any other outstanding balance owed by or to the customer. Please allow 4 to 6 weeks for delivery. Offer available while quantities last.

Your Privacy: Harlequin Books is committed to protecting your privacy. Our Privacy Policy is available online at www.eHarlequin.com or upon request from the Reader Service. From time to time we make our lists of customers available to reputable third parties who may have a product or service of interest to you. If you would prefer we not share your name and address, please check here. ☐

Help us get it right—We strive for accurate, respectful and relevant communications. To clarify or modify your communication preferences, visit us at www.ReaderService.com/consumerschoice.

HP10R

HARLEQUIN®

A Romance

FOR EVERY MOOD™

Spotlight on

Classic

Quintessential, modern love stories
that are romance at its finest.

See the next page
to enjoy a sneak peek from
the Harlequin® Romance series.

Harlequin Romance author Donna Alward is loved for her gorgeous rancher heroes.

Meet Wyatt as he's confronted by both a precious little pink bundle left on his doorstep and his neighbor Elli who's going to show him the ropes....

Introducing
PROUD RANCHER, PRECIOUS BUNDLE

THE SQUAWKING QUIETED as Elli picked the baby up, and Wyatt turned around, trying hard to ignore the feelings of inadequacy as Darcy immediately stopped fussing.

"Maybe she's uncomfortable. What do you think, sweetheart?" Elli turned her conversation to the baby.

"What do you think is wrong?" Wyatt asked, putting the coffee pot back on the burner.

A strange look passed over Elli's face, one that looked like guilt and panic. But it was gone quickly. "I couldn't say," she replied.

"But you were so good with her this afternoon." Wyatt put his hands on his hips.

"Lucky, that's all. I just…remembered a few things." The same strange look flitted over her features once more.

Wyatt took the coffee to the table. "You fooled me. You looked like you knew exactly what you were doing." So much so that Wyatt had felt completely inept. A feeling he despised. He was used to being the one in control.

Elli and Darcy walked the length of the kitchen and back. After a few moments, she admitted, "I haven't really cared for a baby before. The things I thought of were simply things I'd heard about. Not from experience, Mr. Black."

Her chin jutted up, closing the subject but making him

want to ask the questions now pulsing through his mind. But then he remembered the old saying—*Don't look a gift horse in the mouth.* He'd benefit from whatever insight she had and be glad of it.

"I don't really know what babies need," he said. "I fed her, patted her back like you did, walked her to sleep, but every time I put her down…"

Wyatt almost groaned. Of course. He'd forgotten one important thing. He'd been so focused on getting the formula the right temperature that he'd forgotten to check her diaper. Not that he had any clue what to do there either.

Pulling calves and shoveling out stalls was far less intimidating than one tiny newborn.

"She's probably due for a diaper change, isn't she." He tried to sound nonchalant. This was a perfect opportunity. Elli must know how to change a diaper. He could simply watch her so he'd know better for the next time.

Instead, Elli came around the corner of the counter and placed Darcy back in his arms. "Here you go, Uncle Wyatt," she said lightly. "You get diaper duty. I'll fix the coffee. Cream and sugar?"

Oh boy, Wyatt thought, looking down into Darcy's pursed face, his smug plan blown to smithereens. He was in for it now.

Will sparks fly between Elli and Wyatt?

Find out in
PROUD RANCHER, PRECIOUS BUNDLE

Available February 2011 from Harlequin Romance

Try these Healthy and Delicious Spring Rolls!

INGREDIENTS

2 packages rice-paper
spring roll wrappers
(20 wrappers)

1 cup grated carrot

¼ cup bean sprouts

1 cucumber, julienned

1 red bell pepper, without
stem and seeds, julienned

4 green onions
finely chopped—
use only the green part

DIRECTIONS

1. Soak one rice-paper wrapper
   in a large bowl of hot water
   until softened.

2. Place a pinch each of carrots,
   sprouts, cucumber, bell
   pepper and green onion on the
   wrapper toward the bottom
   third of the rice paper.

3. Fold ends in and roll tightly
   to enclose filling.

4. Repeat with remaining
   wrappers. Chill before
   serving.

Find this and many more delectable recipes
including the perfect dipping sauce in

YOUR BEST BODY NOW

by

TOSCA RENO

WITH STACY BAKER

Bestselling Author of
THE EAT-CLEAN DIET

Available wherever books are sold!

HARLEQUIN Presents

USA TODAY bestselling author

Sharon Kendrick

introduces

HIS MAJESTY'S CHILD

The king's baby of shame!

King Casimiro harbors a secret—no one in the kingdom
of Zaffirinthos knows that a devastating accident has left
his memory clouded in darkness. And Casimiro himself
cannot answer why Melissa Maguire, an enigmatic English
rose, stirs such feelings in him…. Questioning his ability
to rule, Casimiro decides he will renounce the throne.
But Melissa has news she knows will rock the palace
to its core—*Casimiro has an heir!*

Law dictates Casimiro cannot abdicate, so he must find a
way to reacquaint himself with Melissa—his new queen!

Available from Harlequin Presents
February 2011

www.eHarlequin.com

HP12972